BIRD
in a BOX

BIRD
in a BOX

BY ANDREA DAVIS PINKNEY

ILLUSTRATIONS BY SEAN QUALLS

LB

LITTLE, BROWN AND COMPANY
New York Boston

FOR
GWENNIE

Copyright © 2011 by Andrea Davis Pinkney

Discussion Guide adapted from *Bird in a Box* Educator's Guide © 2011, 2012 by Hachette Book Group, Inc.

Little, Brown and Company
Hachette Book Group
237 Park Avenue, New York, NY 10017
Visit our website at www.lb-kids.com

Little, Brown and Company is a division of Hachette Book Group, Inc.
The Little, Brown name and logo are trademarks of Hachette Book Group, Inc.

The publisher is not responsible for websites (or their content) that are not owned by the publisher.

First Paperback Edition: February 2012
First published in hardcover in April 2011 by Little, Brown and Company

Educator's Guide prepared by Tracie Vaughn Zimmer

Library of Congress Cataloging-in-Publication Data

Pinkney, Andrea Davis.
Bird in a box / by Andrea Davis Pinkney. — 1st ed.
p. cm.
Summary: In 1936, three children meet at the Mercy Home for Negro Orphans in New York State, and while not all three are orphans, they are all dealing with grief and loss, which together, along with the help of a sympathetic staff member and the boxing matches of Joe Louis, they manage to overcome. Includes author's notes. Includes bibliographical references (p. 273–274).

ISBN 978-0-316-07403-2 (hc) / ISBN 978-0-316-07402-5 (pb)
[1. Orphanages—Fiction. 2. Orphans—Fiction. 3. Louis, Joe, 1914–1981—Fiction. 4. Grief—Fiction. 5. African Americans—Fiction. 6. New York (State)—History—20th century—Fiction.] I. Title.
PZ7.P6333Bi 2011
[Fic]—dc22
2010022851

10 9 8 7 6 5 4 3 2 1

RRD-C

Book design by Saho Fujii

Printed in the United States of America

Let's go, mighty Joe.
Battle like the Alamo.
Hey, hey, mighty Joe.
Time to bomb 'em — there you go!
Go, go, mighty Joe!
Get 'em good — there you go.

ONE

SPEAKY

June 21, 1937

HiBERNiA

FOR CRYING OUT LOUD! SKIP GIBSON, YOU have done it again. You have turned *Happy* Hibernia into *Not*-Happy Hibernia.

How dare you interrupt *Swing Time at the Savoy* to announce the fight. Jeepers!

I'm as eager as anybody to see if Joe Louis wins, but that's a whole day away. It's bad enough that for months I've had to sneak-listen to the reverend's radio. And now that he's finally letting me enjoy my favorite program on the CBS Radio Network, you, Skip Gibson, have squashed it.

The truth is, if the reverend knew I was still thinking about singing — or *swinging* — at the Savoy, he'd lock me in the parish broom closet for a month. But that's Speaky's power. Speaky brings the Savoy to me and lets me dream. Even from the broom closet, I can escape to center stage, thanks to Speaky.

This all began early last summer when the parishioners at our church bought my daddy, the reverend, his brand-new Zenith radio. A gift to celebrate the church's fifth anniversary.

The reverend wasted no time getting to know his newfangled present. That's how Speaky got to be a member of our little family. My daddy even *named* his radio. *Speaky,* he calls it.

Daddy loves Speaky so much that he makes me dust the radio as part of my cleaning chores. Sometimes he watches to make sure I'm doing it right. "Bernie," he says, "give Speaky a rub with the polish, will you?" And there I am, pleasing Daddy, putting a shine to the top of Speaky, as if the radio were a bald prince getting a head wax.

Speaky is perched right next to the writing table the reverend keeps in the closed-off corner of the vestry, the private place where he writes his sermons. That cramped little space is no bigger than a bread bin, though the reverend makes it sound like it's some official office. He calls it his *sermon sanctuary.*

For the longest time, I was not allowed to listen to the reverend's radio. He said he was trying to protect my virtue. But I am no gullible piece of peanut brittle. I know it was more than that. The reverend was right in thinking the radio would get me to missing my mother, Pauline. When my mama left for New York City right after I was born, she hit the road with a heavy suitcase packed full with her big dream — to sing at the Savoy Ballroom, one of the swankiest nightspots in Harlem.

Some days I wish my mother had taken me with her. I guess there just wasn't enough room for me in her overstuffed luggage. But, oh, would I love something else to remember her by. All I know now of my mother is her name, Pauline — and, well, the music on the radio.

That's not much. Especially since I'm left here growing up with the reverend, who, most days, is as starched as the rice water I use to iron his shirt collars.

Sometimes it is no slice of pie being the daughter of the Reverend C. Elias Tyson, minister of the True Vine Baptist Church congregation.

Everybody *adores* the reverend. To his parishioners, he can do no wrong. But in the eyes of my daddy, there are some things that can never be right.

For instance, he knows I can outsing most folks, but my desire to be a big-city performer is bad news to the reverend. It riles him.

Hibernia Lee Tyson is not giving up, though. I'm going to take the dream my mother had for herself and make it come true for me.

Along with Ella Fitzgerald, Chick Webb, and Duke Ellington, someday I will call the Savoy my own. I may have to wait till I'm grown. But if the chance comes any sooner, I will jump on that chance faster than I land on a hopscotch square.

Don't let me admit any of this around the reverend. He has other notions for me. "Bernie Lee," he declares, "places like the Savoy are a hotbed of sinful activity. I believe you've been called to a more fruitful occupation. I feel strongly that you're meant to someday take over as the director of the True Vine Baptist choir."

I don't see anything sinful about singing in a ballroom. Time and time again, I have tried to tell the reverend that to deny me the opportunity to present my vocal abilities to a dance-floor crowd is to trap my God-given gifts under a butterfly net. To me, *that* is a sin.

Everyone in town knows that Hibernia Lee Tyson is going straight to the top. And you can bet your bottom dollar that I have the talent to take me there.

Other than the reverend, there are only two things holding me back. One is my age. I've just turned twelve, which is way too young for the Savoy. But I'm taller than most boys my age, and strong, too. And when I color my cheeks with face powder and use NuNile pomade to smooth my hair, I can pass for being a grown-up lady with real singing experience.

The other thing getting in my way to fame is my stubby fingernails, which I have bitten to the quick. You can't be a big star without nice nails. People love to get singers to sign their cocktail napkins after each show. But who wants an autograph by somebody with fingertips that look like half-eaten pig's knuckles?

The nail biting is a bad habit. No matter what, I can't stop. What makes it worse is all I try that *doesn't* work. I soak my fingers in pickle vinegar. I sit on my hands. I pretend my nails are covered with ants. None of this helps. For the life of me, I can't find a way to quit.

But there's one thing I know for certain. If I were out front at the Savoy Ballroom, I would show everybody that Hibernia Lee Tyson can roll out a tune sweet enough to bake. The world would have to wait for news about tomorrow's Joe Louis fight while Hibernia Lee lit up the airwaves with her song.

The truth is, though, I am no closer to Harlem or the

CBS Radio Network than I am to the moon. I am stuck here in slowpoke Elmira, New York, living upstairs from the True Vine Baptist Church with the Reverend C. Elias Tyson and Speaky, his radio.

Now Skip, don't get me wrong—I'm truly rooting for Joe. So is everybody I know. But *Not*-Happy Hibernia will turn back into *Happy* Hibernia by listening to *Swing Time at the Savoy*. Without interruptions.

But, all right. Seeing as tomorrow is Joe's big night, I guess all I can do is wait. And hope on Joe. And meanwhile, curse you, Skip Gibson, for stomping on my *Savoy*!

WiLLiE

MAMA, SHE TOLD ME TO LEAVE HOME.
And it's just as well, I swear.

I couldn't stay unless Sampson hit the road for good.
Sampson—what a lame excuse for a daddy. *Uh-huh,*
that's Sampson. Nothin' but a sorry sack.

Even after all this time, Lila and the bleach man don't
know I ain't like the rest of the orphans here at Mercy.
That I got a mother and a father, and an address different from this place.

Thing is, though, the house where Mama and Sampson live ain't a real true home. Far as I can tell, you
don't get burnt in a real home. Your daddy don't curse

at your mama in a real home. In a real true home, your mama don't cry herself to sleep, and neither do you.

I get to thinking about Sampson and Mama every time I look at my Saint Christopher medal. And with Joe Louis about to step in the ring, I keep Saint Christopher close as ever. That medal's one of the only things I can say's all mine. Soon as I came here and unpacked my croker sack, Saint Christopher fell out on the floor, chain and all. Before then, the medal ain't seen much of the light of day.

I remember when Mama gave me Saint Christopher. Was my tenth birthday, near to three years back now. Mama, she'd put the little medal in a big box. Covered it all in brown paper. *Uh-huh,* Mama, she's good with making things special.

When I unwrapped the paper and opened the box, the medal was pushed under more crumpled bunches. Wasn't till I dug in the paper and found the small gift, that Mama explained, "It's a Saint Christopher medal. It protects travelers, especially young people, on their journeys."

I turned the little medal over and over in my hand. "Protecting people," I say. "*Uh-huh,* I like that."

Mama say, "And seeing as Saint Christopher was such an important man, I felt he should be housed in a mighty place. That's why I wrapped him so carefully for you, Willie."

When Mama slipped the medal's chain around my neck, Sampson, he started laughing. To him, the whole thing was just so funny. "Why you giving the boy a sissy thing like that?" He was sniffing when he say it. Talking like somethin' smells bad. "How's the boy ever gonna get respect if he's wearing a necklace?"

Sampson gave the medal a tug. Yanked my neck forward at the same time. "I guess you can use all the help you can get, Willie-bo." That's what Sampson called me, *Willie-bo*. He even liked turning my *name* into some kind of joke, funny only to him. That's why I couldn't never make myself call my father Pa. What kind of father laughs at his own son's name? *Uh-huh,* that's stupid, ain't it?

Sampson tugged on the medal again. I turned away from him quick. "When I was a boxer," Sampson say, "my coach told me to get a good-luck charm."

Half the time Sampson spoke, he started by saying, "When I was a boxer..."

But you ain't *no boxer now,* my mind's whispering.

"When I was a boxer, I should've listened to my coach and got me that good-luck charm. Maybe I never would've been saddled with a kid," Sampson say.

Mama, who was busy collecting the brown gift wrap, she flinched.

Sampson wouldn't let up. "Willie-bo, if it weren't for you, I'd still be boxing today — might even be a champ, instead of a outta-work bum with two mouths to feed and a sissy kid who likes wearing jewelry."

"Hush up, Sampson," Mama say. "That medal is a sign of strength."

With the way Sampson's talking about me being a sissy, I wouldn't let myself pay that medal a second thought. I stuffed that sissy thing way far back in my clothes crate, behind my moth-eaten socks.

I kept the brown paper the medal came in, though. *Uh-huh,* kept it. Later, after Sampson had went out drinking, I wrapped the paper around each of my fists, and did me a pair of play boxing gloves. I remember thinkin', *Scrap Sampson. Maybe someday I can be a champ*.

Them gloves was big brown slammers, just like Joe's. Paper dukes that made me feel like a boxing king. Made me wish I had a roaring right fist same like Joe Louis's so's I could knock Sampson out in one punch and leave him wishing he never do mess with Mama or me.

That same night, Mama told me what to do with my Saint Christopher medal. "Tell it your dreams."

Nowadays seems all I do is what Mama say. I whisper my secrets to Saint Christopher. And I wish on that medal every chance I get. Even if it *is* for sissies, it makes me feel good to do it.

I tell Saint Christopher that though I'm long gone from Sampson and Mama's house, I wish Sampson would fall headfirst off the face of the world. And I hope Mama will wake up one day and see Sampson for the sorry sack he is.

Today, since I'm hoping hard already, I won't pass up a chance to put in a good word for Joe.

My wish is short. But *uh-huh,* I mean it:

Let Joe win!

OTiS

WHAT DID THE TIE SAY TO THE HAT?

   Why did the cookie go to the hospital?

   What lays at the bottom of the ocean and shakes?

If riddles could march, tonight would be a riddle parade.

Here they come again. One riddle after another, in a happy line.

They sure are loud this time, a brass-and-drum band pounding inside my head. Playing on my mind, as if Daddy is here telling them himself.

Tonight I speak right to the riddles. I call their answers out into the dark. It's like waving at friends who smile when you see them passing.

"You go on ahead, and I'll just hang around!"

"Because it felt crummy!"

"A nervous wreck!"

That's when Lila comes running. The bleach man is with her. He tries to hush me. He tells Lila, "This boy needs to quiet down. He'll wake up the other children. Is he crazy?"

Lila says, "Riddles comfort Otis. It's just a dream he's having."

The bleach man is shaking his head.

Lila's hand is pressed to her cheek. She's watching me with kind eyes. Her skin is as pink as bubble gum, and smooth under its freckles.

There's nothing smooth or pink about Mr. Sneed. He's as pale as they come. A ghost has more color than he does. That's just one of the reasons I've nicknamed him the bleach man. Like bleach, Mr. Sneed is harsh. He strips the fun out of everything.

Lila's the opposite. She isn't mean. Nobody's bleached her heart.

It's not Lila's way to hush me up. If I ask her one of my riddles, she'll try to solve it, like the last time. She'll think of silly answers, and I'll feel better.

Before I can even stump Lila with one of my riddles, they come back fast.

What did the pig say on the hot summer day?

If you cross a snowball with a shark, what do you get?

Fingers grow on what kinds of trees?

As the riddle parade marches past, I yell out the answers with all I've got.

"I'm bacon!"

"Frostbite!"

"Palm trees!"

Soon the riddles are starting to go. The parade is moving off, and the riddles are gone. Gone till next time.

The thumping in my head is gone, too. But I'm hot as blazes. That's what happens when the riddles come into my dreams.

Lila lays the back of her hand to my forehead. "He's feverish," she tells the bleach man.

She takes a handkerchief from her sleeve. She dips it in the water basin, near to my cot, and wipes the little bit of wet from my face.

Lila knows I'm not crazy. Lila understands. I wish I could tell the bleach man that my mind's all my own. That even though it's near to a year, I'm still missing Ma and Daddy, is all. That sometimes Daddy's riddles still talk in my dreams, is all. Sometimes good dreams.

Sometimes bad ones. And sometimes, when I answer the riddles, I feel good.

That's all. That's all there is to it. Nothing crazy about me.

It's tomorrow's fight that's making me think of Daddy. It's people saying the press will have to eat their statement that boxing will never see a Negro champion. It's the wishing on Joe Louis that's bringing memories of Daddy and Ma back to me so strong.

Daddy believed in Joe. Joe was Daddy's hope.

Daddy believed in me, too. We made a deal, Daddy and me. We shook on a promise.

Now Joe is *my* hope. *My* promise.

If Daddy were here, he'd be putting his all on Joe. He'd be saying a different kind of riddle. He'd be asking a question that won't *be* a question come tomorrow.

What's set to explode while the whole world waits?

The Brown Bomber.

TWO

PROMISES

June 1936
The year before

HiBERNiA

"THOSE ARE HUSSY CLOTHES," PROCLAIMS the reverend.

"Are *not,*" I insist.

My belly is flat to the rug and I'm flipping and folding pages from the Sears, Roebuck and Co. catalog. Like always, the reverend is wearing on my nerves. When we talk, I am *saying* one thing and *thinking* another.

"Sears, Roebuck has only the finest merchandise," I say.

"Fine for gallivanting." The reverend can't help but *declare* things.

Fine for gallivanting, I mimic silently.

I point to a lovely dress with a lace collar and pearly buttons, something you'd see coming in the door of the True Vine Baptist Church on a Sunday morning.

I say, "There's even a rosette on the front. A rosette is not for gallivanting."

I think, *And how would you know about any lady of the night? You hardly ever go out past sundown.*

"Bernie, those catalogs are trouble," the reverend says. "They invite craving. And besides, we cannot afford such things."

"Dreaming don't cost a dime," I say.

The reverend is leaning hard over me. "Dreaming *doesn't* cost a dime," he corrects. "If you ever want the finer things, you'll need to speak properly."

"You're *blocking* the light," I snap.

"Hibernia, you are hardheaded."

I don't say anything.

I think, *Your head is ten times thicker than mine.*

The reverend says, "Close that catalog, and turn your thoughts to spiritual ideas."

I don't budge. The reverend says, "Is there cotton in your ears, child?"

I flip the catalog closed.

I think, *How* did *I get a father like you?*

I huff, "I've shut the book. See?"

I think, *You are straighter than a broomstick and more obstinate than most mules.*

But I won't give up on the catalog so easy. I quickly turn it open to where there are clothes for men. "Look, here's something you might like, a vest with a little pocket for your watch. See the fancy writing on the page — 'Fine Attire for a Man of Distinction.'"

The reverend says, "A true man of distinction doesn't need clothing to prove his merit."

But the reverend is taking a good look at that vest. He even lifts his eyes over the top of his spectacles to see it better.

Before we can butt heads any harder, the reverend slips his fingers into his trouser pocket and pulls out his watch. He looks at the watch's face, then snaps shut the cover, not even bothering to tell me the time.

When he says, "I must retreat to the vestry," I know it's eight o'clock. The reverend is eager to turn on his radio.

"Yes," I say, "time for the vestry."

I think, *I may be hardheaded, but you are* bull-*minded when it comes to listening to that radio.*

I say good night.

"Good night, Bernie," says the reverend. "Don't stay

up too late." He is gone so fast he doesn't even notice that I still have the Sears, Roebuck catalog wide open.

When I hear the crackly radio static coming from the vestry, I know the reverend will not show himself again tonight.

He once told me that he uses his radio only to listen to President Roosevelt's fireside chats. That the radio was "given in God's name," and that his only reason for even accepting the gift from his congregation was "as a means for keeping abreast of the nation."

But honey, that is a bunch of hooey. The reverend is hooked on his Zenith. He insists on listening to Speaky every night, without fail. And it isn't often that I hear the *president* chatting by the fire on that radio.

The truth is, the straight-and-stubborn Reverend C. Elias Tyson has a thing for swing music and the blues. Most nights he tunes in to *Swing Time at the Savoy,* coming live from Harlem.

I go back to my catalog, flipping, folding, dreaming. There are flannel shirts, aprons, long johns, and lingerie. The lingerie is my favorite. All that lace. All those flounces.

When I get to the section marked *Sensible Dresses for Growing Girls,* I flip past fast. I don't waste time with any girl clothes. I need a woman's wardrobe.

I get to page seventy-two, *Ladies' Evening Wear*. The heading says, "For Nights on the Town, and for the Hours that Follow."

There is silk all over this page. There is a pair of shoes made of good leather, with a dance heel and a pretty lattice ankle strap. There's even a fur stole and a hat with feathers. Oh, how I wish the drawings were in color!

I tear out the page with the dance-heel shoes. I tuck it in the bib of my pinafore. *These are my shoes.* I save this page for later, when I will stare and stare at my dance heels, and not spend a dime doing it.

With Sears, Roebuck tucked under one arm, I make my way to bed. When I pass the vestry, I press my ear to the door.

As sure as my name is Hibernia Lee Tyson, I hear what I always hear—the reverend's sermon room secret: Duke Ellington and His Orchestra performing live from Harlem.

I believe the reverend fancies *Swing Time at the Savoy* because he still has feelings for my mother. I would bet a bottle full of dimes that the reverend is drawn to the Savoy's music because he's listening hard for Pauline, trying to somehow catch a hint of her among Duke's orchestra.

Tonight, though, the reverend gives Duke only a short listen. He soon turns his radio dial to a fight between Joe Louis, the Negro boxer, and Max Schmeling, the former heavyweight champ.

Everybody and their brother is talking about Joe. For gracious' sakes, there are a trillion other things to speak on — like what happens to the fur on a stole when it gets wet from when it snows. But stoles and snow are not even part of the Joe conversation. The only thing folks are talking about is that this will be the fight to end all fights. And nobody seems to care about the tough times we're in, either. People are putting down their last little bit of money, betting on Joe Louis. Boo to that! If I had *any* cash of my own, I'd be sending it to Sears.

With all the talk in town, I can't help but wonder what the big deal is. So tonight I listen carefully as Speaky *speaks*.

All I can hear is the voice of Skip Gibson, the boxing commentator, filling up the reverend's tiny room. *"Joe Louis looks overconfident and underweight. Max is coming on strong against the Brown Bomber!...But wait— Joe throws a right! He lands one hard on Max!"*

The strangest thing flings from the reverend's room. It's a whoop, coming out from under the crack of light that draws a line between the door of the vestry and me.

Then a second holler comes louder: "Slam him, Joe! Make us proud, boy!"

There is no mistaking that voice. It's not Skip Gibson roaring out from the radio. Those shouts belong to the reverend. So does the thunder of his foot stomps.

Skip Gibson shouts, *"Joe is still on his feet here in the twelfth round, but Max is all over the Brown Bomber!"*

Another booming clap. Another slam with his foot. "Stay up, Joe!" calls the reverend. "Keep standing!"

Now Skip announces, *"A dynamite right, and Joe Louis goes down! Max Schmeling puts a temporary halt to the meteoric rise of the Brown Bomber!"*

Then Skip delivers more bad news: *"Ladies and gentlemen, on this night, June nineteenth, nineteen thirty-six, history is being made right here. In exactly two minutes and twenty-nine seconds of the fatal twelfth, Joe Louis, hailed the king of fighters, has been counted out. The Brown Bomber has been stopped."*

Right then, Speaky goes quiet from the click of its knob being turned off in one fast snap.

OTiS

DADDY LOVES COCA-COLA. MA LOVES candy bars. But who has money for sweet brown treats? Not Daddy. Not Ma.

"Times are hard," Daddy says.

"No jobs," says Ma.

The president, Mr. Roosevelt, he says these are hard economic days. He says it in the papers. He says it on the radio.

Daddy says it to Ma. Ma tells it to me.

"Don't go asking for things, Otis," says Ma. "Your father's hurting for work."

Even though times are hard, Daddy can always find

a good joke. Jokes that make Ma and me laugh. Riddle-jokes.

"What do you get when a cow is caught in an earthquake?"

"Which building has the most stories?"

"Why couldn't the sailors play cards?"

Daddy laughs and laughs at his own riddle-jokes. He doubles over at the punch lines.

"A milk shake."

"The library."

"Because the captain was standing on the deck."

Daddy's laugh is between a hoot and a snort. It booms from way inside him. So full, he has to wipe his forehead.

Daddy gets me and Ma going, too. Ma laughs big enough to show those gaps in her teeth. I get all choked with laughing when Daddy starts in with his riddle-jokes. They make me run a hand across my own forehead, just like Daddy does.

But sometimes when there's talk of no jobs, Daddy gets quiet, and the riddle-jokes seem far away.

During the day Daddy looks for work. At night he sinks into the *Elmira Star-Gazette*. He shakes his head when he reads about no jobs for people. "When's it gonna end?" he asks Ma.

Ma tries to comfort Daddy. She tries to make him relax by telling him his own riddle-jokes. Mostly it's no use, though. Nothing funny about no money.

There are days when Daddy goes as far as Philadelphia, more than a hundred whole miles away, looking for work. "Philly has promise," he says. But Daddy never comes home with one of those promises.

For months it's been the same. Stale bread is all. Government cheese. No work for Daddy. No promises.

Then, one day, Daddy goes to Philly and comes home whistling. And he's back to wiping his forehead from happiness.

"Daddy!" And I'm happy, too. And wiping my forehead, too. And whistling, too. "Daddy looks good," I tell Ma.

Daddy doesn't even need to tell us riddle-jokes to make us smile. "I've got work!" is all he says. "Good, solid work, operating the elevator at the Claremont Hotel."

When Daddy walks up to the house, he isn't empty-handed. Hoisted on one shoulder is a radio. A proud-looking Philco in a leatherette case. In Daddy's other hand, he's holding some of those Philly promises in a paper sack. A Coca-Cola for himself. A candy bar for

Ma. For me, a whole paper sack filled with packs and packs of Chew-sy Time gum!

"Thank you, Daddy! Thank you!"

After supper we huddle around the Philco. We listen to Joe Louis fight Max Schmeling, all the way from Yankee Stadium in New York City.

The man on the radio tells us what we wish we could see for ourselves, so we can know if it's really true: *"A ripping right by Max Schmeling! Louis is in trouble—he's down!"*

How can Joe be down? All during the fight, I chew my gum, the waxy pieces wrapped like little gifts in colored paper. I know I should make the gum last, but I'm too excited. The chewing helps, so I go for two pieces at a time. I chew till half the packs are gone. *Promise gum,* I call it, hoping that somehow in the chewing I'll help Joe Louis win. But Joe's closer to losing. The man on the radio tells the story.

"Joe is up on his feet, but it's all Max here in round four!"

And then: *"Max keeps pouring it on! The Brown Bomber can't keep it together!"*

And finally: *"Max Schmeling has stomped hard on Joe Louis's near-perfect record!"*

Daddy gets quiet when the fight is over. And even though the day has started all shiny and new, Daddy's face is tight with being sad that Joe Louis has lost to Max Schmeling.

I'm as squashed as my chewed-up gum. I'm twisted up, too, same as the neck on the brown sack the gum came in.

Later Ma tells me, "When Joe Louis fights, it's more than just throwing punches, Otis. That boy's fighting for the pride of Negroes. When he loses, every colored man loses a little piece of his own pride."

I save the chewed-up gum Daddy's brought home for me. I'm holding on to those Philly promises.

At night, I stick the gum to the wall. In the day, I chew and chew that gum. Even when it's dried up, I chew. Even when there's no sweet taste left, I chew. Then I go on to new pieces of gum, adding their sweet to the old wads.

I save the gum wrappers. Different colors those wrappers are—green, yellow, even white. The little squares of waxed paper are a minty memory of Daddy's surprise.

Soon Daddy goes to stay in Philly. To work where there is promise. Before he leaves, he sits me down across from him and Ma.

Daddy says, "Otis, son, I love you and your mother more than I love this life." I can tell by the frown yanking at Daddy's face that he's about to say something important. Ma keeps her eyes on her lap. She already knows Daddy's news.

Daddy says, "The best way to love you is to live where I can earn what it takes to feed you and to keep the four walls of this little cracker-box house around our family. We can't afford to all live in Philadelphia, so I'll go alone."

I nod to show Daddy that I understand. But there's still something sharp coming at me from inside. And my throat is tight with trying not to cry.

Daddy hugs Ma and me at the same time. He tells me to take care of Ma. He tells me that even though I'm just twelve, I'm the man when he's gone.

That's when more promises come. First Daddy gives a promise to me. Then he asks *me* to keep a promise for *him*.

He says, "The Philco is yours now, Otis. I promise you this radio will give you hope." Daddy winds the Philco's cord around its middle and is careful when he sets the radio on my lap. "Promise me you'll take good care of it, that you'll keep it close by listening, and that you'll stay up on what's happening with Joe Louis."

I answer Daddy with a hard handshake, just like a man does to another man. Now it's sealed. We have a deal. It's as firm as his hand squeezing mine.

Daddy explains, "I'll be working long days and night shifts. I won't have time to listen as closely for Joe. I need you to tune in for me, Otis. No matter what happens with Joe, we can believe in him by listening."

The next day, me and Ma watch Daddy go down the road. He walks away with his body bent forward, eager to get to where his work waits. Quickly Daddy glances behind him to see us waving good-bye. He waves fast, then walks. Daddy's steps are slow. He looks back again. It's more than a glance now. Daddy's taking in the sight of us. He holds his hand up to wave once, long.

When Daddy goes, Ma fills the time with cleaning. It's our turn to tidy the alley house we share with the Jenkins family next door. The alley house is hardly a *house,* though. It's a cramped space in the alley, forced between our house and the Jenkins'. A creaky flap door offers only enough privacy to cover the toilet. Daddy's hand-carved sign hangs from the flap-door hinge. The sign says GO AND BE GONE! The alley house isn't the place for leisure. There are seven Jenkins children in all. One of them always has to *go*.

Today is no different. Ma has a tin of carbolic cleaning acid in one hand and a broom in the other. She hands me the broom. "Otis, you sweep. I'll wipe." The two of us can barely fit in the alley house. Before I can even make two swishes with the broom, Petey Jenkins is rattling the door.

"Somebody in there? I gots to *go!*"

"We're cleaning," I call.

Petey yells back, "I can't wait!"

"Hold your horses, Petey," Ma says. "We'll be done soon."

But Ma is taking great care with her cleaning rag. She even wipes the flush crank above her head by the pipe on the wall.

Petey rattles again. "I — I — gots to *go!*"

I tell Ma, "When I'm grown and have money, the first thing I'm gonna buy is my *own* bathroom inside my *own* house."

Ma finishes with her rag. "And when you do, we'll hang a sign that says COME ON IN AND STAY AWHILE."

That night, Ma turns on the Philco. She's quick to find the program she wants — the CBS Radio Network bringing in *Swing Time at the Savoy* all the way from Harlem.

Can my ma ever sing! If she wasn't too busy being my mother, and if she had better dresses and hair not knotted away from her face, she could be one of those Savoy satin doll singers, or Ella Fitzgerald, even.

From this day of holding a wipe-rag, she's still eager for getting dirt off things, and I'm up next. Ma is ready to clean me, too.

Her voice is on the same side of the street as whoever that lady singer is who's coming through the Philco, taking listeners on a jazz ride.

Ma sings along:

> *"Slide back, honey, till I call you in*
> *I want to dive for your love*
> *Take a swim."*

Never letting up on the song, Ma sets our metal basin in the center of the kitchen and fills the tub with warm water from the teakettle. She throws in a hunk of the pinesap soap she's made herself, all the time holding on to the tune, pretty and strong like that Savoy lady.

During the part where only the instruments play, Ma

says, "Wash good, Otis." She turns her back while I sink into the water, thick with the smell of trees. Now I'm singing, too. I can't help it. That's what happens when something sweet touches you. You want some of it. Ma and me sing together, *"Slide back, honey."*

Later, when I'm supposed to be asleep, I curl back the curtain that separates my bed from the kitchen. I glimpse Ma washing her feet in the metal basin. She's dressed in a sleep shirt, a scrub brush pressed to her heel. She works the soap over both feet while she sings along to "Missing Him to My Soles," a song that eases out from the radio Daddy's left behind.

WiLLiE

THERE AIN'T NO MISTAKING SAMPSON'S drill. *Uh-huh,* same warning every time.

"Rise above it, Willie-bo! Rise above it! Get to your feet, boy! I got money on this fight!"

Slick Ricky Tate hooks me good. Throws a left jab that makes me block with my right. Then, when I ain't looking, he hooks hard to my chin, knocks me to the mat. The ref starts counting.

"One...two..."

"Hoo-hah," somebody shouts, "he's down hard!"

"Three...four...five..."

Them voices sound far away. I just wanna lay here and sleep.

But they ain't havin' it. *Uh-uh,* no. Ain't havin' it.

Men, wild as search hounds, hollering and dragging on cigarettes. Dogs acting crazy at ringside, hammering me with screams worse'n Slick Ricky's punch.

Once I'm down, I'm seeing dizzy, and fighting to breathe, and begging my belly to hold on to its supper. No doubt Slick Ricky has busted my nose. I can't smell the chalk on the mat. It's hard to snort back the blood coming in a spurt from my nose. My ears is ringing loud as a noonday whistle. The ref keeps giving me the countdown.

"Six…seven…"

I lift my head. I swallow the hunk of snot choking my throat. I won't never fight to win for Sampson. I fight for myself. I fight for how much I love boxing—for the burst of *oh, yeah* that builds in me when I'm in the ring.

I slam both hands onto the ropes. Yank myself to my feet, quick as I can. But I'm knocked backward by my own swolled-up face, eyes beat up so bad they only let me see through slits. Pounding in my head so hard, all I can think on is pain.

The ref stops counting, but the hollers of them search hounds smoking half-burnt cigarettes keep comin'. The loudest, wildest dog of all is Sampson, my very own father.

"Beat him, Willie-bo! Beat him, so's I don't have to beat *you!*"

Even with Sampson's shouting, my *oh, yeah* is still here. My *oh, yeah* is louder than Sampson's bark. My *oh, yeah* means I'm feelin' good.

Slick Ricky hangs back near his corner. He's grunting and spitting and flinging his big arms over his head. He's declaring himself to be the high-and-mighty kid who gonna be taking home the prize.

But, see, Slick Ricky, he sitting pretty too soon. He ain't learned one of boxing's most important rules: *Nobody's a winner till somebody's a winner.* I move toward him slow, still working hard to get my balance, struggling to see, wincing at every breath.

Sampson's shouts come at me again. "Go for the rebound, Willie-bo! Show him who's boss!"

When I get close to Slick Ricky's corner, I can see enough of his eyes to look him in the face. But he don't bother with me. He's watching the referee, waiting for the ref to call him the winner.

Now I'm sure Slick Ricky Tate don't stand a snow-ball's chance in the sun of beating me. He's turkey-trotting before the slaughter. I know I can land Slick Ricky. I can put myself one fight away from the Copper

Gloves junior title. It's easy from here. *Uh-huh*. Easy. A deep-down voice is telling me, *You can do this*.

Sampson plants hisself at the ropes and keeps adding to the wild mix of hollers. "Get me those copper gloves, Willie-bo! Bring 'em home for me, boy!"

Oh, yeah, uh-huh, it's payday. Time to get Sampson back for the daddy he ain't. Time to snatch the one thing Sampson wants so badly for hisself—a boxing title he can hold. *Yeah. Oh, yeah.*

"*Fight,* Willie-bo!"

Uh-huh. That's when I let Slick Ricky Tate take me out in one punch.

THREE

HOOKS AND CROSSES

August 1936

OTiS

AS SOON AS PROMISES COME, THEY GO.

Daddy shows up from Philadelphia one Sunday. He surprises me and Ma.

"Took a day to join you for church services," he says, pulling both of us into his arms. "I can only stay the day, though. I need to get back to the Claremont Hotel. I'm a workingman now." Daddy is proud.

It is a church day to beat all. We're dressed so fine. I've put on a collared shirt. Daddy wears his best shoes. Ma even takes her Sunday hat down from the shelf. She has a hum rising out from her. She is ready to let the choir hear her joy on this day.

It doesn't take long before Daddy is back to making

us laugh. Back to telling us his riddle-jokes. Back to his old way.

"What sea animal can be adjusted to play music?" This is one of Daddy's favorites.

We all say the answer together: "A tune-a-fish!"

We walk toward our truck, the three of us, arm in arm, step in step. Daddy says to Ma, "Betty, can you lift this boy?"

Ma knows what Daddy's thinking. She says, "On the count of three."

I know what's coming. We link our arms even tighter. We count at the same time. "One…two—three."

On *three* Daddy and Ma lift me at my elbows, just high enough to let my feet jiggle above the grass, and fast enough to scare away the pigeons. We all laugh at the whole silly thing. Daddy says, "In the time I've been gone, this boy has gotten taller. He's still as straight as a clothespin but heavier."

Daddy looks down. "Otis, it must be your clobber feet that are bringing on some extra weight."

Ma giggles. "It's the bricks I feed him."

I say to Ma, "And I'm getting taller from when you hang me out to dry with the laundry after my bath."

Another bunch of giggles springs from Daddy and Ma and me.

As we walk, we come upon a rabbit's nest in the tall grasses of our yard. There's a baby bunny nestled in a pile of brush. "Look," I say. "He's all alone. We could bring him to church. I could show him to people."

I reach for the rabbit, but Daddy stops me. "Come away from there, Otis. You mustn't ever remove a baby cottontail from its nest."

"But he's abandoned," I say. "There's no ma or daddy that I can see. The little bunny's a loner."

Daddy says, "We don't know that for sure, Otis. Mother rabbits leave their babies alone in their nests during the day. They stay away in the waking hours so they won't attract attention from roaming dogs and cats."

Ma knows about bunnies, too. "The mother returns to her babies at night. Let's leave the bunny where he is for now. If his mama's not back after a few days, we'll know he's truly orphaned."

The bunny's fur is just-grown, a fluff-coat of brown velvet. I want to pet him, but I don't.

When we get to the truck, Daddy and Ma ride up front in the cab. I ride in the back on the flatbed where I'd put our radio earlier on so that after services we can listen to music in the church basement and play the radio for the folks who only wish they had a Philco.

This day is so sunny. The breeze blows nice on my face. I have a smile inside, thinking about Daddy's riddle-joke. I tell the riddle-joke to myself, just to make me laugh again.

"Otis," I ask, like I'm saying it for the first time. "What sea animal can be adjusted to play music?"

But before I can say, "A tune-a-fish," I hear a loud horn. When I lean out from the side of the flatbed, there's a hay truck coming right at us!

Then I hear the screech. Daddy's truck rattles and jerks and smacks me against the side of the flatbed.

I call out to Daddy and Ma. But they have no way to hear me from the truck's cab.

Right quick comes the crash.

And flying glass.

And twisted metal.

And a hiss.

Then there's hay flying off from the other truck, dropping on me like rain.

Next come the flames. Loud, high, hot fire, snatching at the hay. Burning up around Daddy and Ma. Sending smoke into the sky. Pouring an ugly odor all over the place. Choking off my breath. Making the happy day go suddenly black.

WiLLiE

THE BOOTLEG'S GOT HIM AGAIN. I SMELL
whiskey soon as he stumbles in the door. Sampson's
drunk as a monkey, second night this week. Man, does
he stink! It don't take a genius to tell he's peed all over
hisself.

He comes in quiet, but the smell. *Uh* — it's so foul, he
might as well be shouting.

He passes by me like I ain't even here and heads
toward Mama, who's at the stove, stirring a pot of
hominy. She also made a heap of corn hash, just for
me. *Uh-huh,* I love Mama's corn hash. And since this
is the night for a Joe Louis fight, Mama's got something else special, too. She wearing her skirt with the

white-white sash that trail down the back. This what Mama call her *fight skirt*.

Mama, she believe that white-white sash is some kind of powerful. She put on her fight skirt every time Joe Louis go into the ring. "To give Joe a bolt," Mama like saying.

I sometimes think that sash was invented by Thomas Edison hisself. It seem to have light inside it. Tonight, it's the most brightest thing in our dim little house. I can spot that sash anyplace Mama's standing, even when she moves to a dark corner to pull a pan or spoon off a shelf. *Uh-huh* — with Mama's white-white sash, and corn hash on the stove, this night sure is good.

Mama don't hear Sampson. She too busy with the pots, stirring the hominy. Checking the lid on the hash. I try to warn her, but at the very same moment I say, "Mama, Sampson's here, and he drun—" Sampson snatches Mama around her waist from behind. Tugs at the back of Mama's skirt sash.

"How 'bout a little kiss, Melva?"

Mama flinches. "Sampson—for goodness' sake, you scared the living wits out of me!"

But that don't stop Sampson from pressing his slob-bery lips to the back of Mama's neck. "Come on, Melva, all's I want is just a tiny taste of brown sugar," he says, puckering up all over Mama.

I mess with the radio, trying to get the CBS Radio Network to come in clearer. Tonight the Brown Bomber is set to fight Jack Sharkey in New York, in Yankee Stadium, in front of more than ten thousand fans. I got all my hopes on this fight. When Joe lost to Max Schmeling, I doubled up on wishing only wins for Joe.

The radio sputters, but I can still hear the commentary. I can still listen to what's happening with Joe. The fight has already started.

Rusty Donovan, the commentator for this fight, he's saying, *"Louis is intent on getting back to being a winner. But Sharkey looks tough here in round two."*

When Sampson backs away from Mama, he tries to speak to her again, but his own belch interrupts. He wipes his mouth with the back of his hand. Then to Mama he says, "You got a-a-a thing—a soft s-p-p-p-ot— for that Brown Bomber, Melva?" His words are a bunch of jumbled-up slur.

Mama shake her head. She won't even look at Sampson. "I got a *thing* for spending time with my son, enjoying the fights," she say.

Sampson cuts his eyes at me.

"Just leave her 'lone," I say.

Sampson's flushed. He leans against the doorjamb. His breathing's short.

"Who asked you, boy?" he wants to know. He burps again, louder this time.

The radio pulls my attention from Sampson. Rusty Donovan cuts through the radio static: *"Louis delivers a barrage of punches! Sharkey goes down!"*

Mama and me are clapping for Joe. "Our Bomber's coming back," Mama say.

Sampson's got a faraway look on his face. For a moment, he's left Mama and me.

That don't hardly last, though. With some drunks, liquor makes 'em irritable. But Sampson, he *always* irritable. When he's full of bootleg, he gets sloppy, too. Tonight, every time he talks, it sound like he got a mouth full of cotton.

He tries to lean close to me to speak, but trips on his own unsteady feet. "Willie-bo, I can s-s-see why you'd want to lis-s-sten to Joe fight. Seems lately that kid is a loser, just like you."

I don't say nothin', but I'm hot mad. When Sampson's tight from drinking, best to lay low till the drunk in him wears off. So I act like I don't hear what Sampson's saying. I keep messing with the dial on the radio. Even with the static, it's clear Joe's in good form tonight. Rusty Donovan sounds pleased. He say, *"The Brown Bomber comes out in round three looking very confident."*

Sampson starts talking real loud so we can't hear Rusty Donovan's commentary. He won't let up on putting me down. "Willie-bo, you ain't nothin' but a shame," he say. "My boy — the kid who likes laying around in the ring."

I stay quiet. I'm feeling like a bird in a box, wishing I could fly free of Sampson's ugly ways. Wishing I could lift myself straight outta here.

It's hard to keep myself together. *Uh-huh,* real hard. But then I think of Joe. Right now. In the ring. Solid. Giving his all to flatten Sharkey. And I remember what I know from boxing. Sometimes the best fight is no fight at all. Even a bird in a box can get free if he uses his wits, if he don't ram at the walls around him.

So I don't give Sampson the satisfaction of getting into it with him. It's like they say, if you don't wanna fight, don't get in the ring.

But when Sampson starts back in with Mama, holding myself together ain't so easy.

"What you cooking for me, Melva? Something I can dare to eat, I hope." He looks in the pot of hash on the stove. That good-good corn smell is the only match for Sampson's liquor stink. Then Sampson gets busy with the hominy, stirring it.

Mama knows the same thing I know. Don't give Sampson the time a day when he's drunk.

"You can eat it," she says simply, her back still to Sampson.

Instead of wearing off, seems the liquor in Sampson's blood is hitting its stride now. "*Eat* it—*ha!* Melva, I'd be better off eating my shoe."

Sampson comes up behind Mama a second time. "Melva, since I can't eat your cooking, why don't you just give me some more sugar to sweeten my tongue, to pay me back for all the bad meals you've slapped on a plate and tried to pass off as food."

Now Sampson's got Mama locked up in both his arms, hugging her and trying to smooch more on her.

"Sampson!" Mama jerks away. But Sampson, he a big man. Even with her fight skirt, Mama ain't no wider than a laundry post next to him. She can't shake Sampson.

Rusty Donovan is shouting Joe's success: *"Blistering punches by Joe Louis! A right! Sharkey goes down!"*

Up to now, I been using all I got to steer clear of Sampson.

But enough's enough.

Two strange, strong things happen at the same time. I cheer for Joe by grunting his name. *"Joe!"*

Soon as I say it, I feel Joe's power somehow helping me fight.

First I try to pull Sampson off Mama, but even with whiskey running through him, Sampson's got the strength of two men, the grip like a bulldog's.

But Joe's still here. Holding off Sharkey.

I use what I know from the ring—*jab, strike, block*—but none of that works on Sampson. It's like raindrops trying to knock out a grizzly bear.

I start fighting like a girl. I claw and claw at Sampson's back. I scratch his face. I kick him in the shins. *Oh, no, I'm starting to slip. Nooo…oh, noooo…*

But soon I don't care if this *is* a softy's way of fighting. It's this or let Sampson run us over like the freight train he is.

Sampson turns away from Mama long enough to consider me. I shove my knee into Sampson's privates. He bends sharply at his middle. I've stunned him good.

"Don't mess with Mama that way!"

Pain's got a grip on Sampson. He licks his lips real quick. He's slow to speak. "I'll mess with *you,* then," he say, all cocky.

Rusty Donovan's still holding my attention.

"The Bomber has sent Sharkey down hard! The ref is counting! One ... two ... three ..."

It's looking like a victory for Joe, but I can't celebrate it.

No, *uh-uh,* can't celebrate.

Sampson pins both my hands, heel-to-heel, in just one of his steel fists. He pulls me toward the boiling pot of hominy. In his other hand he's got me by the scruff of my neck, same way you do to a kitten. He sure ain't treating me like no little pet, though. He pushes my head way down in the hominy pot till my nose ain't no more than a hair away from the boiling white.

Rusty Donovan's shouting, *"Can Sharkey weather this storm? He's up at the count of six!"*

My face, it's hot and wet from the steam. Rusty Donovan gives the blow-by-blow on Joe: *"Louis goes back to work, measuring his man — hitting to the body and head!"*

I'm trying to buck Sampson, but I'm afraid that even the tiniest move will put me closer to the hot grits. I can't seem to call Joe to me now. Joe's up, but I'm down for the count. *Nooooo…oh, nooooo.*

"You hungry, boy?" Sampson's asking. Even from behind me, I can smell the liquor lighting up Sampson's breath.

It's a good thing Mama answers for me. I'm so scared, my voice won't come.

"Sampson, *don't!*" Mama cries.

The radio commentary follows up right after Mama speaks. Joe's winning.

"A tremendous left hook! Sharkey goes down. A clean knockout by the great Joe Louis! The Brown Bomber is on the rebound!"

Then, in a single shove, Sampson presses my hands into the scalding white mix. He holds 'em down in the thick hominy.

My eyes do a wild dance under their lids. My skull twitches with pin sticks of pain. When my eyes dare to open for only a second, I'm looking up into the face of my father.

I'm crying…screaming…burning and begging, all at the same time.

"Nooooo, Sampson! Noooo!"

Sampson staggers out the back door.

Mama runs to me. She helps me to the water pump at the side of the house. Cranks that pump's handle fast as ever. The water is cool on my hands.

It's dusk. Fireflies are playing tag all near us. They's tiny sparks on the air.

I can't tell what's spilling faster. Mama's tears, mine, or the pump's water.

It don't matter whose is fastest. I let all the wet run.

Mama hugs me to her, holding on and letting go, too.

"Willie," she say, "you've got to leave here. When Sampson comes back, you need to be gone."

"But, Mama—"

"Mind me, now," she say. "There's a place called Mercy. Go tonight."

"Come with me," I plead. I'm whimpering like a little kid, all soft again. I work the back of my burnt hand over my eyes, trying to press down on so much little-kid cryin'.

"No, Willie," Mama say. "I've been thinking about this, long before tonight. And now I know it's right. This is about you, and your good."

I don't argue with Mama. *Uh-uh*. Can't. She's set on me leaving.

We go back inside, where Mama bandages my hands. Tells me how to get to Mercy. "If you walk at a clip, you'll get there by morning."

She packs me a tin of hard bread and corn hash.

Saint Christopher, he's around my neck. Right then, I know all I got is me. Me and Saint Christopher.

Mama kisses the medal, then both my cheeks. Everything is all blurred up, from how I can't stop cryin'. The only thing even a piece clear in this night is the white-white from Mama's fight skirt sash.

Mama's wiping the wet from my face with her sash. She's working hard not to cry, too. She say, "Get on now, Willie."

I back off slow, still seeing this all in a blur.

"Bye, Mama."

I get to Mercy from hitching a ride on a hen truck. "Here's where you get off, boy," the driver say, and swerves away in a swell of his own dust.

It's Lila who welcomes me at the intake table. "Come," she say softly, and pulls out a chair for me. "Rest."

She's looking sadly at my hands. But she admits me without even a question. Takes me for an orphan, I guess. Truth of it is, I take *myself* for an orphan now.

Lila unwraps my bandages. "They've become dirtied," she say. "You'll heal better if air can get to your hands."

I nod. *Uh-huh,* I know this from the ring. Bruises go down faster when they ain't covered.

"I'll bring some salve after you're settled," Lila say. I'm waiting for her to ask me where I come from, and who got me here, but she don't. She works silently. Seems Lila don't have to ask nothin' about me. Seems she knows things already.

She gives me a pair of cottons, and shows me to the ward, where the other kids is asleep. My bed is under a low crossbeam. I hang my Saint Christopher medal right over my pillow so I can see it first thing when I open my eyes in the morning, last thing before I close 'em at night.

My first days at Mercy are hard, hard going. Slow, not thinkin'. Only feeling the skin on my hands sting as they heal.

I'm still rattled by Sampson's ugly ways, still messed up from knowing that because of my hands, I can't even get in the ring to *lose* a fight. Even with Lila's kindness, I'm still sick with so much hate I can see just one thing — that my boxing's gone.

The only thing hurting more than this is what's left of my swolled-up fingers.

HIBERNIA

IT'S A SIN TO GOSSIP IN CHURCH. BUT sometimes you're sinning before you even know it, and once you get started, it's hard to stop. Today is one of those times.

I lean close to Carla Wright, the girl who stands in line next to me in the True Vine Baptist Youth Singers choir. Our choral group has just sung the opening hymn. I don't turn my head to speak. Real gossip is done by talking out the side of your mouth.

I whisper to Carla without hardly moving my lips. "Her skin is the pretty color of bone china. But she is no kind of bony."

Carla whispers back the same way. She says, "And

china, *well,* I suppose that is better left to daintier types."

Now I'm tempted to keep up the gossip with Carla. Or else I could pray to be delivered from this temptation. After all, I *am* in church. But, oh, is it ever fun to talk from the side of your mouth. I promise myself to go on with Carla only a little bit more. *Then* I'll pray.

This is the third Sunday in a row that plump lady's been here. I spotted her last week, and the week before, but didn't take a good look those times. Now that she's back again, I'm all eagle eyes.

Carla's eyes are as sharp as mine. She's not praying, either. "Have you noticed that she pays close attention to every word coming from the pulpit?" Carla whispers. "Have you seen how she sings every hymn? And when the reverend asks for an *amen,* she doesn't miss a single one."

All right, Carla's leading me down the gossip trail. It's too hard to turn back now. So I pray. *Forgive me, Lord, this is too good to stop.*

I press toward Carla. "She's the only white person ever to set foot in our church. That lady stands out like a lump of sugar in a pepper patch."

Yes, Lord, forgive me. I curl my bottom lip under my

top one to halt myself. But I'm still watching. And I'm gossiping in my mind, which, to my way of thinking, is only half a sin.

Aside from bone-china skin, the lady's clothes on her last two visits to True Vine gave her away as a stranger. A moss-colored dress and flat-as-mud-pie shoes are *not* Sunday best. And to make it worse, when she first came to our church, she wore brown woolen socks — the same brown as the mud pies — rolled at her ankles like somebody plopped a doughnut on top of the mud pie.

Every churchgoing Baptist knows that when you arrive at the Lord's house, you come dressed in your finest. Even in these down-and-out times, folks can always manage to shine at True Vine.

My eyes turn to Roberta Wilkins, who gives the term *Sunday best* its full meaning. When I see Roberta in town any weekday selling her little bitter apples, she's dressed in the same brown shift and half-cracked shoes. But come Sunday, the woman shows off a peach-colored dress with a ruffled collar and pumps with a dance heel. And before you see the powder rising off Roberta, you can smell its gardenia fragrance bouncing on the breeze.

Being the reverend's girl and a member of the True

Vine Baptist Youth Singers choir, I also wear my very best to church. My Sunday dress is periwinkle gingham. I would not be caught dead in ruffles or the smell of gardenias.

My church shoes are the same shoes I wear every day of my drab life — poop-colored tie-ups. I try to spiff up my shoes by shining them with castor oil. Grease somehow helps them look more dressy.

There's nothing shiny about the white lady, though. Everything she wears is dark and sensible.

The reverend's taken notice of her, too. It's a clergyman's job to know his congregation. And you can best believe the reverend doesn't miss a thing. I see him watching her as she slides into the pew. When he gives his sermons, his eyes rise over the top of his spectacles to get a good look.

For the past two weeks, that lady has shown up, doughnut socks and all.

But today something is different about our visitor. This being the third Sunday of the month, it's Baptism Sunday. Carla's back to gossiping. "That lady's dress is as yellow as the morning," she observes.

"It's got flower-petal cap sleeves, too," I say. "They show off her copper-colored hair, and those freckles."

The reverend is all full of enthusiasm on Baptism

Sunday. He addresses the congregation with so much glory. "If you are moved to be baptized today, please stand to show your conviction."

Wanda Clark is the first one out of her seat.

"Praise God," says the reverend. "Our first follower has taken her stand for the Lord."

"Amen," says Wanda, who is smiling with all her teeth.

Lester Williams stands up next. But he isn't smiling. His head is down. His shoulders are up by his ears.

Lester's wife, Kit, has been on him to get baptized ever since she found a shelf of John Barleycorn whiskey stashed in their woodshed.

"Brother Williams is ready!" exclaims the reverend. Now the reverend points his sausage finger right at poor Lester.

"He's *been* ready," says Kit, who's outgrinning Wanda Clark.

"Who will join these brave souls?" asks the reverend.

A short silence drops down on all of True Vine. The reverend surveys his congregation. "Great occurrences come in threes," he says. "Which one of you will move toward greatness today? Who will be brave enough to stand?" The reverend is back to pointing. This time he's using his whole hand, sweeping it over the air in front of him.

Suddenly a voice comes from the third-row pew. "I believe it was Joshua who said, 'Be strong and of good courage.'"

It's the white lady! Carla nudges me. "Hibernia, look. She's raising her hand like a volunteer for a bake sale." This time when Carla speaks, she doesn't even talk sideways.

"I will be your third candidate," says the lady proudly.

Now the silence that settles on the congregation is as long as a mile. Everyone's got their eyes on this stranger. Even Lester Williams picks up his head to see better. I'm watching and waiting and wondering.

The reverend looks pleased. As he does each Baptism Sunday, he invites all parishioners to be baptized to join him at the pulpit, where they will lead the procession to the muddy cradle of water at the edge of the land where True Vine stands.

In most churches, folks get baptized by dipping in the river. At True Vine, we baptize by standing at the bank of a gulch. We in the youth choir sing "Wade in the Water." All those getting baptized dip their feet in the little bit of wet that rests in that ditch.

The white lady goes first. She takes off her shoes and doughnut socks. At least the socks are white today. But, oh, her wide feet. I whisper to Carla, "Onion bunions."

The lady lets her callused toes soak a whole long time, while everybody sings. And when we get to the part of the hymn that says, "See that band all dressed in red / It looks like the band that Moses led," she presses both palms toward the cloudless sky.

Soon after services end, Onion Bunions approaches the reverend as he is greeting parishioners who flow from the church's narrow front door.

"Reverend Tyson, good morning."

The reverend takes her hand. He shakes it enthusiastically.

"My name is Lila Weiss."

"Mrs. Weiss, hello."

Others are in line behind her. They eagerly await the reverend. He is a popular man.

"Reverend Tyson, seeing your youth choir sing this morning has touched me so."

The reverend chuckles from far down in his throat. "That is the whole point of worship, Mrs. Weiss — to be moved in some way."

"Reverend, I work at the Mercy Home for Negro

Orphans. The children at the orphanage are in so much need. It would bring them such cheer to hear your youth choir sing. I know it's a ways off, but perhaps this holiday season your choir could perform a Christmas concert. A few selections from your holiday canon would go a long way in spreading goodwill. It would make the children so happy."

Right away the reverend answers. "Yes," he says. "Certainly. A Christmas concert for the children at Mercy."

The reverend gives a slight nod. While bowing his head, he glimpses the lady's doughnut socks. His eyes return quickly to meet her gaze. They are still shaking hands.

That night I ask the reverend about a word the lady used when stepping forward for baptism. "What is a candidate?"

The reverend says, "One who is worthy."

OTiS

I HAVE THREE THINGS LEFT FROM DADDY and Ma—gum wrappers from the time Daddy brought me a treat, Daddy's Philco radio, and an embroidered hankie stitched by Ma. I keep the gum wrappers in one pocket, Ma's hankie in the other.

I take the radio with me wherever I go. Somehow that small box keeps me remembering Daddy. The brown leatherette case is the same color as Daddy's skin.

Tonight I have the radio quiet as a whisper.

Maybe that kid likes radios, too, because the first time I see him, he's got his eye on my Philco. His cot is near mine, and he's watching me. Lila has just come on to her shift. The sky is still black, even though morning will be here soon. That kid is wearing white cottons, the sleep shirt and pants they give us children.

Lila and the bleach man are at his cot. When he talks, they listen close, and pay even more attention when he shows them his hands.

His hands are solid flesh. Heavy, but they can dance. They push the air when he speaks. They bob and fly in front of him. He uses his fists to show what he's saying.

I shift on my cot to see more for myself. I get a closer look at his hands, puckered with cracked black skin.

One hand *isn't* a hand. It's still got most of its fingers, but it's a stump, is all. No fingernails. No thumb.

The other hand, it isn't much better. The pinkie and the ring finger look sewed together. The other finger, his pointer, is only half there, forming a claw.

I don't want to gawk, but my eyes keep stealing, once, twice, then daring to go back a third time. I make my way to his cot and sit gently on its edge.

The kid offers the bleach man one of his hands. The bleach man's own hands hurry to hide in the pockets of his pants. So the kid turns to Lila, who doesn't shy away. She gives his curled hand a shake. Just like that.

Like she's meeting the mayor. Turns out, she knows this boy already. "This is Willie," she introduces.

All's I can think to do is cup my hand over his. It's knitted skin stretched across crooked knuckles.

I tell him, "I'm Otis."

With my palm on top, he pumps his stump fist once to give a shake.

Later, in the dayroom, Willie's sitting in one of the chairs made of paint-chipped metal. He's perched at the window, looking out on the back lawn of patchy grass and dandelions.

All he does is stare. But he's watching something, too. Something only he can see. Something that makes his eyes shift. Seems he's watching a memory pass in front of him.

A smile plays on his lips. Then a wince tugs at his face, and he shakes his head. Something's gone all wrong.

He mumbles a bunch of gibberish, talking to the lawn. I can barely hear, so I move closer. He says, "The peanut bag got to cryin' when it saw me coming. Used to be, I could hook that bag dizzy. *Uh-huh,* I could hook it. Same way I could hook in the ring."

While he talks, he rocks in his chair. His shoulders sway forward and back, close to the window glass.

I pull one of my own chairs next to him. My radio is in my lap, with the cord pulled to its fullest to reach the wall outlet. *The Lone Ranger* is on. Silver, Lone's horse, is galloping Lone away from danger. I set the radio down on the floor.

This Willie kid doesn't even notice me sitting by him. At least he doesn't let on if he does. But when Silver gallops back, the kid's eyes turn to see the radio.

He keeps talking words that don't make sense. This doesn't bother me, though. I guess whatever he's saying makes sense to him. The same way my riddles make sense to me.

His hands are talking right along with him. The hand with the sewed-up fingers stays close to his face. The stump hand has a mind of its own. It punches the air with a sure rhythm.

Willie sees me then, smiles a little. He looks glad to have another kid nearby. I move closer. I don't have a clue what Willie's saying, but I nod once to show him I'm listening. *Go 'head.*

He says, "Soon as I stepped between the ropes, folks was calling my name. They was wanting to see my hook. They was hollering, 'Hook him, Willie! Hook him good!' Folks was betting their last dime on Willie Martel's hook."

Now both his hands go wild in front of him. They are two quick-witted crows, working together. One hand helps the other.

"Hooks and crosses could've taken me all the way," he says. "Hooks and crosses, they was my ticket. I could snap out the lights of any kid who dared fight me. I was gonna be a champ. I could've had the Copper Gloves junior title in my back pocket. *Uh-huh,* could've had it tucked tight. Down in my pocket."

The chair legs make tiny screeches on the floor tiles. Those dayroom chairs aren't meant for rocking.

Willie's breath paints gray steam on the window glass. Then something in his voice changes. His talking drops to a whisper. His words get tight. "Sampson hated my hooks and crosses. He hated that I was on my way to the top, while he was falling fast. I was a contender in line to be a champ, but he was a sorry sack, standing in the bread line."

Willie's rocking fast. I'm not scared he'll tip the chair. *He needs to rock,* I think.

His hands have fallen to his lap. Something's shot down those fast birds. Now they're heavy hooves, slow to move, quiet as he speaks.

A little tin medal hangs from a chain around his neck. There's a holy man on the medal. He's holding a little kid, helping that child get to where he's going.

When he speaks again, he touches the medal. "Them copper gloves was mine," he says. "But Sampson wanted 'em for hisself. That's why I threw the fight. That's why I gave the title to Slick Ricky Tate. To make Sampson pay for being so greedy."

I still don't understand what Willie's saying, but I'm listening close, anyhow.

He presses his forehead to the window. He squeezes his eyes shut. "But Sampson, he won in the end. He took my hands. Stole 'em from me," Willie says softly.

When his eyes open, he turns them from the patchy grass to me. His eyes are set in a wide, dark face. It's by looking back at him that I see. He's about my same age, just bigger.

Willie sets his messed-up hands on both my shoulders. He says, "Otis, I'm a boxer gone bad."

FOUR

SEEDS

October 1936

OTiS

I'M SWEEPING THE FRONT HALL WHEN
Lila comes in. The bleach man doesn't speak to me. He
frowns, is all. Guess he can't even say good morning.

Lila's hugging a pumpkin in both her arms. The
bleach man squints. The steam that puffs out from
your lips in cold weather escapes the bleach man's
face.

"Mrs. Weiss?"

"It's the perfect day for carving a jack-o'-lantern that
all the children can enjoy," she says.

"Mrs. Weiss," he says, "decorating for Halloween is
not your job. You are here to facilitate the children in
their daily routines, to make sure they are clean, fed,

and free of afflictions such as head lice and ring-worm."

The bleach man always finds something to pick at for no real reason. He's good with criticism. This never bothers Lila. It seems she can always see it coming and knows how to meet it. Today is no different. She's looking like there's something to be happy about.

"Mrs. Weiss, you've been employed here as an intake and maintenance worker for just a few months. I knew well enough when I hired you that you had never worked with children in an *official* capacity. But you seemed very efficient and strong-willed. These are good qualities for keeping children in line, and the reason I thought you'd make a good employee here." He's got his eye on Lila's pumpkin.

"Mr. Sneed, as efficient and strong-willed as I am, the truth is, I love children."

"But do you have the ability to *monitor* children?"

"As you have seen, I have a special way with young people."

The bleach man's thumbs are tucked at his belt. "Other than your so-called way with young people, can you keep them out of trouble? Do you have any children of your own?"

"I'm not lucky enough to have had children."

"Then how do you profess to know what it takes to fully supervise young people in an orphanage?"

"Mr. Sneed, when we first met about this job, I never *professed* to know anything. But I'm very attentive. And children like me." Lila nods in my direction. She's right. I like her.

"Mrs. Weiss, this job is not about having kids *like* you by doing things such as carving pumpkins. Some of the children who come here arrive with emotional problems. Others can be unmanageable."

"Mr. Sneed, they're orphans. It would seem to me that they're in need of someone to—"

"Mrs. Weiss, if you don't mind me saying so, you're a rather, well, portly woman. Do you really think you can continue to handle the demands of this job? Walking two flights of stairs to get from the entrance hall to the dayroom to the central sleeping ward, changing bedsheets, cleaning the latrine, preparing food..."

"Mr. Sneed, I'm handling things just fine. Even the portliest people can climb stairs and cook. And if you don't mind *me* saying so, Mr. Sneed, you could stand to become a bit more portly yourself. There isn't much meat on your bones."

I slow my broom to listen better.

"Mrs. Weiss, I find your humor unfavorable."

"Despite what people say, Mr. Sneed, we portly people aren't very jolly."

"Mrs. Weiss, have you taken a close look at the shingle outside? This is the Mercy Home for Negro Orphans. There is little appreciation for wisecracking in an orphanage."

Lila shifts the pumpkin to rest it on her hip.

"Mr. Sneed, have *you* taken a look past your shortsightedness? The children here might become more amenable if they're allowed to have more fun."

Her eyes are square on me now. So are the bleach man's. My broom is as still as the air in the room. I have stopped pushing the floor crumbs back and forth. All's I can do is blink. "You—back to work!" the bleach man snaps.

"What about books and games? Do the children ever read? Does anyone ever *read* to *them*? Do they *play,* Mr. Sneed?"

"Read, Mrs. Weiss? Play?"

"Books, Mr. Sneed. *Oliver Twist, The Secret Garden, Alice in Wonderland.* And games, such as hopscotch, Simon Says, Chase Your Shadow?"

"Mrs. Weiss, you speak as if this is the Social Club of Elmira."

"Good grief, Mr. Sneed, *you* talk like this is a detention home for misbehaved kids. What about interacting with others? Do the kids here ever come into contact with children who aren't orphans?"

"That's not advisable, Mrs. Weiss."

"Mr. Sneed, as far as I can see, any child with no parents has done nothing to deserve bad treatment. No child, whether an orphan or not, should be deprived of a good book, the company of all kinds of children, and some cheerfulness."

I beg my broom to keep sweeping so the bleach man doesn't give me a second thought. This is better than *Fibber McGee and Molly* on the radio. All's I really want to do is listen.

"Mrs. Weiss, you are tenacious and opinionated. Can you use those virtues to work with the children here in a way that is best for them and for the overall good of Mercy?" Lila sets her pumpkin down on the rickety intake table.

"Mr. Sneed, *you're* the one who's tenacious and opinionated. Can you just trust me enough to let me work with the children who live here in the way I want?"

"Mrs. Weiss, by hiring you, I gave you an opportunity. Please don't give me reason to regret my generosity."

"Mr. Sneed, I've always been grateful for the chance

to work here, especially in these times. I find regret a waste of energy. So I'll give you no reason to indulge in it."

I don't know even half of the big words between Lila and the bleach man. But I know what hopscotch is, and Simon Says. And I sure know what it means to arm-wrestle. Lila's gone wrist-to-wrist with the bleach man, and she's won.

The bleach man huffs off. He's shut his trap for now. Lila sticks out her tongue after him, curling her hand around an army knife, just pulled from her apron pocket.

She spreads pages from the *Elmira Star-Gazette* at the base of her pumpkin, and waves me over. The pumpkin's a beauty, perfectly rounded and evenly colored.

Lila pats the stool next to the intake table. I settle beside her.

"That's *some* pumpkin," I say.

"Halloween's not far off," says Lila. "The best way to keep spooks away from our doorstep is to present them with a jack-o'-lantern," she explains.

My eyes are fixed on the pumpkin.

Lila gets right to work. She presses the knife's tip firmly into the pumpkin's top to make a jagged circle. As soon as she releases the knife, I've got both hands around the pumpkin's stem. I yank off the lid with a single tug. I'm quick to look down in, eager to get the pumpkin's surprise.

"Seeds!" I say. "Let's get the seeds." And right away we're taking turns scooping out the stringy globs of pumpkin flesh that are laced with the pumpkin's goodness. Lila's brought an empty canning jar for the orange slop.

I slide a cotton hankie from my pants pocket and spread the square of white on the table in front of us. Embroidered initials are stitched onto the corner of the hankie, two proud letters in green: *BR*.

"What lovely crewel work," Lila says.

"My ma made it," I tell her. "It's all I have left of Ma."

Lila motions with her chin. "Whose initials are those?"

"Betty Rollins. That was Ma's name." I smooth the hankie on the table next to the pumpkin.

"Ma loved dried pumpkin seeds. She used to set them out on the windowsill so they could dry in the sun." I get to remembering, and it feels good. "Then

Ma'd salt the seeds, fold them in her hankie, and bring them when we went to church, so we'd have a snack on the way home. Those salty, crunchy seeds sure are tasty. And the hankie makes them a special little gift."

We pick the seeds one by one from the jar and set them to dry on the newspaper. There are enough to make a small seed hill.

"We'll be crunching all day," I say.

Lila's holding her army knife with a sure grip. She's ready to carve the jack-o'-lantern's face. "The more spiky the teeth, the better," she says.

I say, "Let's give his nose a high point."

Lila sure can carve. I put the lid on the jack-o'-lantern's head and step back from the table to look. "That pumpkin looks so happy. Who can he scare with a grin like that?"

"He doesn't look frightening to you?" she asks.

I shrug. "Nope."

"Not all jack-o'-lanterns are meant to ward off evil, Otis."

"What are they for, then?"

"Some invite happy spirits."

I wrinkle my eyebrow. I get to thinking. I ask, "Can this pumpkin invite Daddy and Ma?"

Lila doesn't answer. She's quiet, is all, adjusting the pumpkin's lid. She seems to be thinking, too.

I say, "Daddy had an army knife like that one you've got there." Lila holds the knife out in her palm to give me a better look.

"Daddy could carve all sorts of things—toothpicks from a twig, checker pieces, even wooden whistles," I say.

Lila sits back in her chair, listening.

My little smile is starting to grow. I like sharing these memories with my friend. "My ma carved our pumpkin every year, then dried the seeds."

A chuckle finds its way out from me. "Daddy did all the crunching," I say.

Lila folds her knife and tucks it back in her apron pocket.

Then she does something that sneaks up on me. She takes both my hands in both of her hands and gently keeps them there.

"Good memories are for holding," she says.

HiBERNiA

WHEN I WAKE UP AND SEE THE FROST ON my window, I thank heaven for the favor. A cold day means I can wear my woolen coat without a question from the reverend. It's the perfect cover-up for the Sunday dress I've got on underneath.

I've hot-combed my hair and slicked it with NuNile. With the wind blowing the way it is, I wear my plaid kerchief. The kerchief surely won't give me away, and it'll keep my hair in place.

If the reverend bothers to look at my legs, he'll know something's different about me. I'm wearing a pair of stockings from Roberta Wilkins.

I have never wanted a Saturday like I want this one.

Today Smooth Teddy Wilson, one of the swingingest piano players and bandleaders in all of New York, is holding auditions for a lead singer. As the reverend would say, the Lord has blessed me with a divine co-incidence. Smooth Teddy Wilson's tryouts are at the fairgrounds, in the central pavilion, just across from the relief truck, which comes to the grounds every Saturday at dawn.

As good timing would have it, I go to the relief truck every Saturday, anyhow, to gather food rations for parishioners who are too old or too sickly to stand in line. So, to the reverend, today is no different from any other.

But this morning I have a plan. I will gather up my food rations quickly, then head over to the pavilion to show Smooth Teddy Wilson that Hibernia Lee Tyson means business.

The reverend's got his nose stuck in his newspaper.

"I'll be back before noon," I say, pulling at the tails of my kerchief that hang under my chin.

The reverend doesn't even look up. "Get some scrapple," is all he says, and I'm out the door. Like always, I bring my wagon so I can carry home a new hunk of government cheese and a fresh block of Oleander butter.

Today my wagon seems heavier somehow. Even empty, it's harder to pull. It could be the frost crunching beneath its wheels that slows it down. Or it could be the wind, or the clouds that have turned the sky to dirty mop water.

Or maybe it's my conscience that's heavy. Telling the reverend a half-truth is like carrying a sack of sand.

The food lines here in Elmira snake from the relief truck's tailgate to the edge of the fairgrounds. Today I'm one of the first in line. The only folks ahead of me are those who sleep on the grass the night before the truck pulls onto the muddy patch where it parks.

When I get to the truck, I'm behind a mother and little boy and two toothless hobos. After me, the line grows and grows as people gather.

Mr. Haskell, who drives the truck and rations the food, is always glad to see me. Today his truck hatch is already open when I walk up. Mr. Haskell is sitting on top of a cheese crate. There are barrels and boxes all around him. He smiles big at the sight of me. "Well, look at you, Hibernia Lee Tyson." He notices my stockings. I don't give the stockings any attention. I just act natural.

He loads my wagon with three crates of cheese, two tins of Oleander butter, and enough scrapple to feed all of True Vine for seven Sundays. Then he adds four cans of condensed milk and a burlap bag of Liberty sugar. "Here's something extra for the sweetest girl in town," he says, securing the sugar between the crates of cheese.

I do my best to be grateful, but I'm cursing the extra stuff that's weighing me down. When I move off the line, my wagon will hardly budge. I tug at it with all my muster. I get the wagon to turn its wheels, but it's slow going.

The central pavilion is up ahead. There's a line of people winding off the front, a line double to what is trailing the food truck. Even from far away, I can see that it's mostly women waiting to meet Smooth Teddy Wilson.

If it weren't for my wagon, I'd be in that line quick. But it's taking me three forevers to get to the pavilion. It doesn't matter that there's frost under my feet. I'm panting like a dog in the desert.

I'm not even halfway there when icy raindrops land on my knuckles. I try to pick up the pace, but the crates and butter and burlap hold me back. The raindrops call all their friends and soon it's a downpour.

My hopes droop faster than Roberta's stockings. I'm soaked before I can think on what to do.

The reverend has said that all true prayer is asking. But my thoughts are so jumbled, I don't even know the right questions. I start chewing at my thumbnail.

Should I leave the wagon behind? Or should I forget my dream and go home?

My kerchief comes loose. The NuNile in my hair starts to drip. The rain even finds its way into my pockets. My poop-colored shoes are one with the mud that is turning them a whole new shade of brown.

At the pavilion I see a parade of umbrellas. If I can just get to the line, maybe someone will share. I turn my back to where I'm going and pull the wagon hard with both hands.

My wagon's gone stubborn on me. It's stuck. The mud's got us glued to the center of the fairgrounds at the wide-open place between Mr. Haskell's food truck and Smooth Teddy Wilson's tryouts.

I am no crybaby, but right now all I can *do* is cry. My tears don't even seem to wet my face, which is dripping with rain. My kerchief has become a limp collar around my neck. The stockings are a puddle all their own. I bite off two fingernails at the same time.

I'm drenched from my bangs to my toe jam. I'm crying so much, my shoulders shake. I sniff hard to keep from bawling, but a loud *uhhhrrrooooeee!* howls from someplace in me that's cracking open. Before I can stop it, one *uhhhrrroooeee* follows another — fast, then faster. *Uhhhrrroooeee! Uhhhrrroooeee! Uhhhrrrooooooooooeeeeee!*

The only dry patch on me now is my sheet music, pinned to the lining of my coat.

When I finally make it home, I slink quietly in the back door. The reverend calls from the parlor, "Bernie, is that you?"

I manage to call back the one thing I know will keep the reverend in the other room. "I got the scrapple."

WiLLiE

IT'S LONG PAST BEDTIME. ONLY LIGHT
there is coming onto the ward is from one bulb hanging on a wire in the latrine. That bulb's got a yellow
face and is shining just enough for me to see Otis's
radio, which is turned way, way down.

"Where you get that?" I whisper.

Otis answers real soft. "From my daddy."

"It's a Philco, ain't it?" I know radios.

Otis nods. "You want to hold it?"

I sit up on my cot.

"Just don't let the bleach man see it."

Otis's talking like he's warning me about something.
He tells me how he nicknamed Mr. Sneed.

"You sure named him right, Otis," I say. "He's just *like* bleach — stings your skin, strips away anything colorful, is pale as a pillowcase."

When Otis settles his radio onto my lap, that brown box sure do feel good resting on me. It's all warm. Got quiet voices rising out from the little speaker holes. I'm running my hand over the radio's case. Even with the twists of skin that cover my fingers, I can feel the heat of Otis's radio.

Otis pushes his chin toward my lap. "Go ahead," he says. "If you turn the dial, you can get the Jack Benny show."

I'm thinkin', *My blasted hands.*

I say, "*Can't* turn no dial — my fingers won't —"

Otis, he don't waste no time. He's quick to help. He turns the radio dial for me. He gets Jack Benny right away.

"My daddy loved Jack," Otis says.

Jack Benny's voice is coming from the speaker holes. *"So I go to the doctor, who tells me to lay off the cigars. The doctor insists that if I keep puffing, my life will become unmanageable. I say, 'Doc, cigars relax me. If I don't keep smoking, my wife will become unmanageable.'"*

Otis's shaking his head and laughing. The radio's

hum grows on my lap. It sends a good feeling through all of me.

Jack Benny is on to a new joke, another one about a doctor. *"Do you know why the bumblebee went to the doctor?"*

A second man's voice comes out of the radio. *"No, Jack,"* he says, all lively, *"why did the bumblebee go to the doctor?"*

Otis and Jack Benny say the answer to the joke at the same time. *"Because he had hives!"*

Otis repeats the joke's funny part. *"Because he had hives!"* That gets me to start laughing.

Jack comes back with another joke. A second one like a riddle. And more about going to the doctor.

"Hey," says Jack, *"did you hear about the steak knife who went to the doctor?"*

Otis, he starts laughing all over again. *Uh-huh,* his whole bony body's laughing. If a whittle stick had a twin, Otis'd be it. The widest part of him is his mouth when he's laughing. All full of beaver teeth pushing past lips too small to hold 'em back. A two-door gate pressing partway open. He got a skinny head, too, topped off with an acorn's-cap of hair.

Otis finishes Jack's joke before Jack can even say the part that's gonna make us all be laughing.

"He had to go—he was all cut up!"

Something about the way Otis's giggling with his throat catches onto me.

I say, "'All cut up'—*uh-huh!*" Now the two of us, we snickering together.

"You sure know some jokes," I say. "How you get to be faster than Jack?"

"From my daddy," Otis say.

Them other kids from the ward stir on their cots. Otis turns the radio down to a low growl. All we can hear now is Jack Benny coming through as a mumble. I can still feel every time Jack's telling a joke. Something in his joke-telling voice makes the radio's sound roar up on my lap.

Lila, whose shift ends soon, peeks onto the ward from the hall. "Boys—hush up!" she whispers loudly.

Soon happy band music's leaping out from the radio. Then comes a man's voice, telling us to buy Genuine Jell-O with the extra-rich fruit flavor. Telling us our satisfaction is guaranteed. Then more music's coming. The Jell-O man say, *"With Genuine Jell-O, you're in gooood taste."*

Otis reaches behind his pillow and slides out what looks like a little croker sack made from a hankie.

He unties the bundle, folds open my warped-up fingers, and drops in a bunch of something.

"Pumpkin seeds," he explains.

I put my hand to my mouth. Throw in them seeds.

Them seeds are crunchy, pumpkin-sweet. I'm chewing and nodding and smiling, all at the same time.

"Tastes good," I say.

Otis, he do like me. Takes a handful of seeds and chews 'em up.

Lila, she back again, filling the doorway.

Otis empties the last of his seeds into my bent-up palm.

His whisper is quiet as Lila's shadow. "*Gooood* taste."

FIVE

BIRD

December 1936

HiBERNiA

IF THERE'S ONE THING I CAN'T STAND about the holiday season, it's that the reverend insists his church be clean from top to bottom. So here I am, dusting, making sure the reverend's leather-bound Bible is properly positioned on the pulpit.

My dust rag is wrapped tight around my fingers. I go for every crevice. The Reverend C. Elias Tyson is a stickler for cleanliness.

I even dust the Bible's back cover. When I flip through the book's pages to unsettle any dust there, I come to a picture of a beautiful lady tucked in the Bible's gutter. The picture is nestled at Luke 2:1–20, the story of the birth of Jesus, the passage the reverend draws from every year for the sermon he gives the Sunday before Christmas.

There's an inscription on the picture.

It says:

> *To C. Elias —*
> *Honey doesn't get much sweeter than you.*
> *Love and kisses,*
> *Pauline (Your Praline)*
> *July 10, 1923*

My face gets hotter than a straightening comb, and I'm curling my toes inside my shoes.

Honey? Sweet? The reverend?

I know right away I'm looking at something that isn't meant for my eyes. Yet here are the eyes of Pauline Tyson, my mother, looking back at me. They're the same eyes as mine, dark pennies.

I don't know whether to smile, or cry, or curse the reverend.

I have asked him about my mother a trillion times.

A trillion times the reverend has said, "She's gone, Bernie. No need knowing about her."

A trillion times I have asked for a picture of my mother.

A trillion times the reverend has said, "All Pauline left behind was her memory."

The photograph is dated the year before I was born and is signed on the reverend's birthday, July 10.

This picture is more than a memory. It's a secret the reverend has been keeping from me. In finding the reverend's private birthday gift, I am meeting my mother for the very first time.

Mama's hair is pressed and styled, and beautiful. It is the soft petals of a rose curling in around delicate cheekbones.

Even in a photograph, there is only one way to describe my mother's skin. *Satin.*

I lift the picture from the reverend's Bible, resting it in my palm, scared as a hick at a queen's tea party that I will somehow break it.

Mama's smile is full of kindness, just like those penny eyes. I can't help but stare.

Something inside me starts to hum with a strange joy. I'm trembling, and breathing so fast. My heart is a hammer. This must be what stage fright feels like.

My legs won't even let me move. I lean against the pulpit, then back up toward the piano bench, where Mrs. Trask, our choir accompanist, sits every Sunday. I will not take my eyes off Mama. I would give up blinking if I could.

I'm sitting but still as wobbly as the bench legs beneath me. I trace Mama's face with my fingers. My fingernails are raggedy patches against Mama's skin.

Soon I hear heavy footsteps, and Mr. Straight-as-a-broomstick roaring.

"Bernie — Bernie Lee! Where *are* you?"

Now that hammer near my ribs is doing double time. I swallow hard.

The reverend doesn't see me right away. I'm blocked by the pulpit.

I wish I could eat Mama's picture. That way, I could hold her inside me forever. Instead, I pick at the nails on each of my thumbs.

The reverend calls me again, louder this time. *"Hibernia!"*

I ease the picture underneath my thighs, then slide myself closer to the keyboard and do my best to play "Do, Lord, Deliver Me." I am not even halfway through the first bar when the reverend comes up from behind. He's holding the dust rag I've left on the pulpit.

I'm no Fats Waller on the piano, but I can plunk out a tune good enough. So I keep playing. This is the first time ever I am thankful for my chomped fingernails. They keep my fingers pressing the piano keys smooth and steady.

The reverend knows the song I'm playing. He says, "The Lord will *deliver* you when you *deliver* on your chores."

I'm quick with an explanation. "I took a break from cleaning to practice my piano."

The reverend lifts his spectacles to peer at me. "You can brush up on your piano tomorrow when Mrs. Trask comes to rehearse the youth choir for a Christmas concert at the Mercy Home for Negro Orphans."

"What *Christmas* concert?" I want to know.

"Mrs. Weiss, our new parishioner since last summer, has asked that we oblige her by performing for the children at Mercy, where she works."

Then I remember Baptism Sunday in August, when the lady with onion bunions asked about us singing at holiday time.

I look back over my shoulder at the reverend. "That was *definite*?"

"Yes, Bernie, and it would please her to hear our youth choir sing for the children at the orphanage."

I work hard to keep from sucking my teeth. Mind you, I will never turn down a chance to sing, but wasting my voice on orphans is a true shame.

The reverend can tell by my arms folded tightly that I am not glad about having to sing for a bunch of orphans. "What kinds of kids live at Mercy, anyway?" I ask.

"Bernie, it's time for you to *show* some mercy. Many of those children have no parents. Some of them have been left by parents who can't take care of them. Others find their way to Mercy on their own when they cannot tolerate their troubled homes."

I keep my arms folded. "So—some of the kids *have* parents?"

"Yes, Bernie."

"Do they *have* an appreciation for good singing?"

The reverend answers by telling me that I *have* no choice in the matter. "You and the choir will bring those children some much-needed holiday spirit."

It's no use protesting the reverend, so from here on in I hold my tongue. But the whole time I'm wishing Smooth Teddy Wilson would come back to Elmira and take me away from this piano bench and the True Vine Baptist Youth Singers.

The reverend rests the dust rag on my shoulder. "Now get back to work," he says before he's gone.

On Sunday, I'm seated behind the pulpit with the rest of the choir, while the reverend starts up his sermon. I can see all the members of True Vine. Every face in the place is looking up at the Reverend C. Elias Tyson.

I watch the reverend from behind. His thick shoulders force the seams of his black suit. As soon as the reverend turns to Luke 2:1–20, his whole stance changes. All of him goes tense. His hand clamps the back of his neck. Here we are in this chilly church, and the reverend wipes his nape with his hankie.

He keeps on with his sermon, but his delivery isn't as smooth as it is most times. He flips the crinkly Bible pages while he says, "Glory to God in the highest, and on earth peace to men on whom his favor rests."

The congregation doesn't seem to notice anything strange about the reverend. Like always, they're hanging on to his words like a child holds a rope swing. But I know the reverend isn't his true self. His hand and his hankie have not left the back of his neck.

The reverend is looking for his picture of Pauline. Mr. *Sweet Honey* is trying to find his *Praline*.

Even more luscious than a praline is knowing that the reverend's picture of Pauline is hidden under my bed pillow, bringing me honey-sweet dreams.

OtiS

THEY LINE UP IN THE DAYROOM, HOLDING
a banner.

True Vine Baptist Youth Singers.

I spot her right away. She stands out from the rest.
Her voice rises higher than the others'. Straight to
heaven, that voice goes. Up, up, until it reaches a place
only angels can touch. She doesn't have to work at it,
either. She just sings, is all, and it comes out sweet.
Same as how I feel when I watch her.

Who is she? I wonder. *This girl with a gap-toothed
smile and skin the color of peanut butter.*

With a voice like that, you'd think they'd put her out
front. But she's stuck in the back, behind a bunch of

shorter kids who don't sing half as good. From the second row, the girl's notes fly forward and rest on me.

Her hair is a cottony bundle of plaits, woven close to her small round face.

Her hands keep easy time to the music, patting at her skirt with each beat.

I'm watching and listening, and remembering what joy is.

She knows joy, too. I can see it rising out of her when she sends up a high note.

She catches me staring. Her dark eyes drop to the floor but come back at me quick. She smiles then, and keeps her gaze on mine.

Now I'm stuck on looking at her, and I can't stop. All my attention belongs to this girl.

I know what's got me glued to her.

This girl looks like Ma, only younger.

When the choir is done, the lady at the piano says to her singers, "Please, children, introduce yourselves to your audience."

I'm forward on my chair, waiting to hear who she is. Before her comes Carla, Robert, and Fay. Then, finally, it's her turn. She tells us her name with so much pride. She makes sure we all hear it.

"Hibernia Lee Tyson," she says, real clear.

Hibernia.

A name as pretty as the music she makes.

Hibernia Lee Tyson.

Unforgettable, is all there is to it.

Later I ask Lila, "Do you know anything about girls?"

Lila has to think on that one. "I'm an *old* girl," she says. "What *anything* do you mean?"

"How do you make a girl smile? A young girl, near to my own age?"

"Smile first."

I ask, "What do girls *like?*"

Hard thought is pinching Lila's brow. She's really trying to help me. "Thoughtfulness. Sincerity. Humor. Gifts."

Good, I think. *I've got at least some of that, but not all.*

"What if you don't have money to buy a gift?"

"Gifts are about giving what's most dear to you, Otis. The best gifts don't cost money."

"What if the girl seems like somebody who wants fine stuff?"

Lila is clear on her advice. "Follow the Three-S Plan," she says. "First, make your gift *sincere.*"

I'm paying close attention. The second *S* is "When somebody makes your heart beat a little faster, act *soon* — before you lose your nerve."

"Who said anything about my heart beating fast?"

"Otis," says Lila, "I'm an *old* girl, not a blind one."

I ask, "What's *S* number three?"

"*Sweet* presents are always appreciated."

Two days before Christmas, Lila takes us kids to Hibernia's church, True Vine Baptist. Before we get there, I press those three *S*'s into my memory — *sincere, soon, sweet.*

We meet up with Hibernia at the door of the church. We're going in at the same time. She's noticing my big boat feet. I press the toe of my right boat over the toe of my left, trying to make them seem smaller somehow. Up close, Hibernia's a chin taller than me, and just as pretty as I remember.

The organist is playing "O Come, All Ye Faithful."

She says, "Hi," is all.

"Hi," I say.

She's still got her eyes on my shoes. "I hope Santa brings you new feet for Christmas."

I'm so busy looking at her face, as smooth as a pond, I don't even have anything to say about my feet.

We're blocking the door. People scoot around us, eager to get inside, where the music and the church are warm. Lila's gone ahead with the others, who are all in the fourth-row pew.

I want to show this girl there's more to me than boat toes. I blurt a riddle. "What did Mrs. Santa say to her husband when he asked her what the weather would be on Christmas Eve?"

Hibernia looks puzzled. "What kind of harebrained question is *that?*"

Then I remember the rule of telling a riddle. The rule of telling a riddle is that you have to first *tell* the person you're *telling* them a riddle, or else the riddle comes out *ridiculous*.

"It's a riddle," I try to explain. "See, I like telling rid—"

But it's too late. Hibernia doesn't wait for me to prove that too-big feet are only part of what makes me special.

"Ask Santa for some smarts, too," she says, then winks.

All's I can do is follow Lila's Three-S Plan, be *sincere,* and tell her the riddle's answer.

"Rain, dear."

Hibernia's thinking on it. She's putting it together. She folds her arms tight, but she's giggling a little. *"Rain, dear,"* she repeats.

"Rain, dear," I say, proud and happy with my sincere self.

Hibernia says, "You're a goof-head." She pushes one foot toward me. Gives me a little toe kick. "A goof-head with goofy shoes and harebrained questions," she says.

Sincere — heck. The first *S* doesn't work!

Another *S* comes quick — *scared*.

I worry I won't get the chance to give Hibernia the gift I've brought in my pocket.

My heart is pounding faster than a jitterbug dance contest. I jump to the next *S* — *soon*. I got no time to waste. Hibernia's friend is calling her over.

I reach past my pocket's mending stitches and find the gum. I hold it out to her in my palm. "For Christmas" is all I can manage.

Hibernia considers my offering, first by lifting it, then by sniffing. She says, "It's rude to turn down a present. Especially so close to Christmas. Thank you."

Before *I* can thank *her,* her friend is calling out in a loud whisper, *"Hibernia, come sit down."*

The service is about to start. I join Lila and the other kids from Mercy.

Hibernia slides into the first-row pew on the end. I can see her from a sideways view.

Her daddy, the Reverend C. Elias Tyson, is giving the longest sermon I've ever heard. Something about believing in miracles. I'm struggling to pay attention. I can't let up from watching Hibernia, and praying for a miracle of my own.

That's when I get *my* Christmas present from Hibernia Lee Tyson.

She's secretly unwrapping my gum. She fakes a yawn to sneak the gum in, and starts chewing slowly. By the look of it, I can see the gum's flavor spreading onto her tongue. For a quick blink of a moment, Hibernia closes her eyes to really *taste* the gum.

The final *S* in the Three-S Plan comes true right then. Watching this angel is so, so *sweet*.

She cuts her eyes in my direction.

She gives me the best *S* of all — a *smile*.

The whole walk home, I'm as warm as a radiator, even though it's starting to snow.

Then I remember. I never once told Hibernia Lee Tyson my name.

WiLLiE

CHRISTMAS IS FOR FOOLS. WHO ELSE BUT a fool would believe in wishes that don't come true?

I learned my lesson about Christmas a long time back. Don't expect nothin'. Don't be a chump. Not even tonight, Christmas Eve, when everybody else on the ward is sleeping tight, dreaming of sugarplums.

Even Otis thinks some kind of magic gonna happen. "There's always a surprise on Christmas," he say before he turns over on his pillow. Poor Otis. He's one of them Christmas saps.

Tonight Otis falls asleep fast. Got his radio on low.

"O Tannenbaum" is floating out from the speaker holes. No voice, just the music.

Sleep don't come easy to me tonight. I'm on my back, watching up at the crossbeam over my head. The cotton sheet and blanket on my bed is scratchy from the lye they use to clean our linens. They too thin to keep me warm. Not big enough to tuck me in.

There's water trickling through the radiator pipes, but ain't none of its steam heating me.

It's thoughts of Mama that won't let me sleep. Thinkin' on her keeps wakefulness knocking on my mind with a heavy fist. I wonder, *Is Mama spending this night with Sampson? Or is she sitting alone by her radio, wondering if that sorry sack's gonna be coming home?*

Mama, is she missing me? Wishing I was there to keep her company, while she listening to "O Tannenbaum"? Is my mama alone with her own sugarplum wishes?

This being Christmas, I miss Mama especially hard. I'm glad for Saint Christopher. That medal, it keeps me focused, same way I concentrate on the peanut bag when I'm training for the Copper Gloves junior title. Saint Christopher, he's a place to put my eyes. A way to keep sight of what's right in front of me. A way to not look behind, or ahead, especially when I do like Mama once say, when I wish on Saint Christopher every day.

Tonight I send up a special plea. *Uh-huh,* an extra-special kind of prayer. I sure hope Mama's Christmas is a good one.

The radiator hisses its steam, and soon I'm asleep.

Later, when it's way deep in the night, a tinny *plink* wakes me up. A soft metal tapping sound comes from the rafter above my bed.

Plink. Plink. Plink.

With the light from the latrine, I see a shadow dancing on the beam. A glint from my Saint Christopher medal flashes and juts from under the light. The tinny sound stops. Saint Christopher swings on his chain. I'm watching real careful. The tinny sound, it comes back.

Plink. Plink.

Something's hitting at Saint Christopher. Something's making him jerk and bob. But all of a sudden the motion halts. I don't look away from the chain, not once. And soon the chain is back to jumping. And with each *plink, plink, plink,* a white patch flings out from the dark place above the rafter.

I get to my knees to take a closer look. When the white flashes again, I see it's a paw. A cat's paw, striking a jab.

I stand up quick on my creaky cot. That cat and me, we come face-to-face.

The cat startles. His eyes is tiny lanterns in the shadows. They's fierce, but scared, too.

"Hey," I whisper, and I reach for him. But he ain't havin' it. He throws that paw at me fast. He lands a mean scratch right by my brow. Now *I'm* the one who's startled. I ask the cat, "Where you get that jab?"

He answers by hurling his other paw, harder this time. "Just like Joe Louis," I say. "A righty. *Uh-huh,* a mighty righty."

I take the medal down off its nail. I sit cross-legged on my cot, dangling Saint Christopher on his chain in front of me.

The cat wants to keep at the medal. He prowls along the beam. He searches me with them lighted eyes. He watches Saint Christopher. Then, in a single pounce, he's on my lap, going for the medal.

He jabs twice more with the pads of his paw. His eyes, they dart with each swing of Saint Christopher.

Every time his paw hits the medal, it makes the tinny *plink, plink*.

This cat, he smaller than most. Not a kitten, but not full-grown, neither. He's a kid like me. Now that he's close, I can see all of him. Both his front paws are snowballs of power. The rest of him is black as the night outside.

"I know fighters with all kinds of punches," I tell him. "But you the first I seen who got white gloves."

Even with his strong jab, this cat been beat up. His coat's shabby. He's missing patches of black where something's snatched at his fur. The ugliest place is behind his ear, where a scab has stopped new fur from growing.

The cat's hind leg is bent, like it's healed wrong from being broke. "Who tore you up?" I ask.

The cat has a hard time sitting still. I try to settle him, but he gnaws and claws hard at my knuckles. "Sorry, cat," I say. "I win this round. You can punch all you want. The skin on my hands is dead leather. I can't feel nothin'."

He studies me. He's listening.

"Where's your ma and daddy at?" I ask.

He steps in circles at the foot of my bed. He answers with a tired *meow*.

"That's what I thought," I say. "No folks. A stray. Well, stray, you in the right place. Most of us here ain't got no real family. And we all been hurt."

The cat comes to my lap. He noses my medal and chain, which is jumbled up in the well made by my folded knees. He can't help fighting, though. His claws go for the chain, ripping at my cottons. Since the skin on my legs wasn't burned, I can feel his scratches. But I let him go ahead. He needs to fight. It's what comes natural to him, I know.

The cat drags my chain in his pointy teeth and goes back to his place at the end of my bed. He finds comfort on the thin blanket. When I put my finger to the fuzzy spot between his ears, he purrs and purrs. *Uh-huh,* he thrusts his head for more. Suddenly I remember the bird in a box who gets free by giving up the fight.

"Even a stray needs a name," I say. "And I got just the name for you — Bird."

In the dim light, I can see the scratches he's made on my hands. They's puckered lines where he's broken my skin. But them scratches, they'll heal.

Finally, Bird settles himself. He rakes his belly with his tongue. I put my pillow at the base of my bed, and sleep with my feet against the bed's iron bar that's supposed to be at my head.

The radiator is back to hissing. I feel warmer now.

I sleep, holding Bird till the silver light of Christmas dawns.

SIX

WRAPPER CHAIN

January 1937

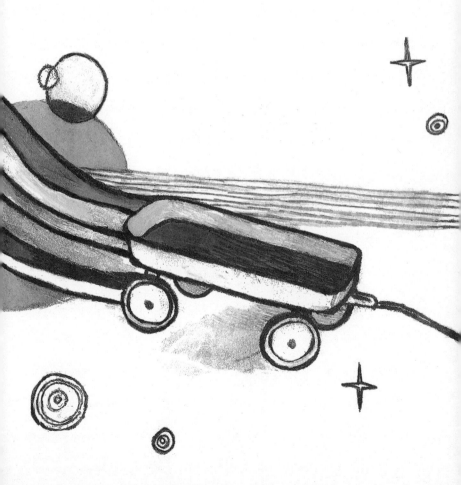

OTiS

I SAY TO WILLIE, "YOU KNOW THAT GIRL who came here singing?"

"What girl?" he asks.

"The girl from the church choir, Hibernia. Hibernia Lee Tyson."

"Who?"

How could Willie forget that singing? I remind him of the True Vine Baptist Youth Singers and their Christmas concert, and how Hibernia Lee stood in the back and had the best voice of all.

Willie nods. He remembers now. "That pretty-skinned girl with the singing that goes high up."

"Her," I say.

"I saw you talking to *her* at True Vine."

I tell Willie about giving Hibernia the gum but forgetting to say my name to her. "Still, I'm sweet on that girl," I blurt. I have never told a soul about this. I feel it even more when I say it.

The words fly out from me a second time. "I'm sweet on Hibernia Lee Tyson."

Willie shakes his head. He's got a smirk. "Sound like you announcing good news."

"Love *is* good, especially when you show it."

"How you gonna show that girl you love her? She don't even know your name."

From my pocket I pull a handful of gum wrappers. I've been saving those wrappers. When Ma and Daddy were here, those wrappers were full of shiny promises. Now the sweet is chewed away. But memories can be sweet, too. I think on Daddy and Ma every time I sniff the minty smell of those colored paper squares.

"I'll show Hibernia I love her with *these,*" I say.

Willie says, "Most girls I know don't get soft from a pile of paper."

I don't even answer Willie. I just line up the wrappers, is all.

White. Yellow. Green. Yellow. Yellow. White.

The order doesn't matter one way or another. But already the crumpled bunch is a parade of color.

White. Yellow. Green. Yellow. Yellow. White.

I crease each paper strip, one at a time.

Willie looks like he's seeing magic.

"Where you learn to do that?"

I pull the paper parade taut to build a gum-wrapper chain.

"From my ma," I say. "Once, after my daddy left Ma and me to go back to his work, Ma told me we could pass the time until Daddy came back by making a wrapper chain. Ma showed me how."

Willie says, "She sure *did* show you."

"I can show *you*," I say.

Willie shakes his head. "Can't," he says. "You need fingers that work for folding."

I say, *"Try."*

Willie gives the creased paper strips a hard look. There's eagerness in his eyes. The little squint on his face gives it away. He's wanting a challenge. He says, "I'll watch while you do it," but he's leaning in, and focused. So I push.

I say right back, *"I'll* watch while *you* do it."

"Gum chains are for sissies."

"Be a sissy, then." I line up four wrappers in front of Willie.

White. White. Green. Yellow.

Willie's ready to curse. "Give a green one."

I put a green in his left hand, and another green in his right.

Willie holds them with his sewed-together fingers and his stumpy thumb. He licks his lips. "How I start?"

I put my hands over top of Willie's. I guide him in the folding. Together we tuck the first two pieces. The link is lopsided. Willie's jaw goes tight. "Let's add the next one," he says.

It takes our four hands to weave the paper squares. Two more links and Willie's got the start of his own wrapper chain. "How I tuck it good like yours?" he asks.

"Keep at it," I say.

Willie reaches for more wrappers. "I want to add some yellow."

I cradle my hands around his again. But he nudges me off. "I'll try myself."

I go back to tucking the links on the chain I'm

making for Hibernia. I try to keep my eyes on my own wrappers. I try not to tell Willie what to do.

His work is slow. His weaving takes time, one link to my four. He stops to give his hands a rest, then starts up again.

"Good, Willie. Real good."

WiLLiE

BIRD, HE FOUND HISSELF A GOOD PLACE
to sleep. Got his little black body curled up between
two joists that support the rafter above my cot. Never
knew cats could snore. But my cat, he got a motor saw-
ing out from him. *Uh-huh,* sure do snore, that cat.

Lights-out is long gone. Otis and me, we both awake
as the day, waiting for the fight to start between Joe
Louis and Bob Pastor. The sound from Otis's radio is
low. The speaker holes is sending out faint crackles. I
shove my cot closer to Otis's. For Joe, I listen sharp.
Uh-huh, my ears are all for hearing Joe Louis.

The man in the radio says to not turn the dial. Joe's
fight is coming soon.

Bird's snore got a whimper mixed in. Wonder if he's havin' a bad cat dream.

"Otis," I whisper, "how you on secrets?"

"Good as anybody, I suppose."

I lift Bird off the rafter. I bring him down between Otis and me, right near my pillow. Bird don't even wake up. His snore is keeping a quick rhythm.

Otis's mouth falls open. He's surprised. He smiling, too.

"Can I touch his head?"

"Try not to wake him," I say.

Otis pets Bird's ears with two fingers. Soon the cat's whole body's humming. He's warm like Otis's radio. Like the Philco, he sending a buzz into the dark room.

"I named him Bird," I say, and I tell Otis about the bird in a box.

"Bird," Otis say real soft, never letting up on petting with his fingers.

"What happened to make him so raggedy?"

"He a stray," I say. "He been beat from alley living. He a fighter, too. Probably picked his share of fights. Got knocked back a few times."

Soon as the man in the radio tells everybody he's broadcasting live from Madison Square Garden, Bird starts to stir. When the radio man announces Joe Louis and the crowd hollers, Bird's eyes open to slits.

"This is it," whispers Otis, "the fight!"

Otis sets his Philco on his lap. I settle Bird onto mine.

A commentator I don't know shouts out from them speaker holes. His voice, it's a blade, slicing through the static:

"Live as a wire from Madison Square Garden, this fight is the talk of all talk. I don't mean turkey talk, either. I mean talk about folding money. Tonight's winner stands to earn thirty-six thousand smackers! Will that money go in Joe Louis's pocket? Or will Bob Pastor be the richer man?"

Bird hears the fight. He juts one of his cotton-ball paws, then wakes with a start. He don't stretch or yawn like most cats. He's full awake. Up on all fours, footing around on my stretched-out legs, prickling the blanket with his claws.

Otis looks worried. "You woke Bird."

"He woke up hisself," I say. "This cat loves a fight. He don't wanna miss Joe."

I'm eager for the match to start, but tonight there's all kinds of commentary 'fore they ring the bell to get going on round one.

"We have a Jimmy Johnston fight here, ladies and gents — a match arranged by the Boy Bandit himself, one of the craftiest promoters in the business, who tonight is representing Bob Pastor, Joe's opponent. The rumor mill has been churning out a story that says Jimmy booked this fight to make the Brown Bomber look bad in the ring with his man."

My fists are firm to my thighs, *pressing* and *rubbing*. I rock to keep from punching. If I start trying to fight alongside Joe, I might lose track of what's coming through the radio.

"Hear that, Otis? Jimmy Johnston got Joe this fight with Pastor. Pastor, he that college fighter who went to New York University. He smart, but he ain't—" Otis say it 'fore I do.

"He's not tough like Joe. Besides, nobody can make Joe look bad," Otis says.

Finally the start bell dings. The man in the radio tells us what everybody in Madison Square Garden can see:

"Joe comes out strong with his signature right! He lunges fast at Pastor! He goes for a solid strike. But Pastor's good at ducking and weaving. He's got Joe running after him."

Now Bird's prowling from my cot to Otis's, back and

forth. Bird goes from jabbing at the speaker holes of Otis's radio to scratching at the patches on my blanket.

It's harder than hard to keep from wanting to fight, too. Fever's coming to my hands, making my thighs go warm as I *press, rub, press*.

The fight's unfolding but staying the same for Joe:

"The Brown Bomber is getting a workout tonight. Not much punching here, just a lot of keeping up with Pastor's fancy footwork. Joe Louis is not used to this kind of fight. Joe's a boxer, not a runner. It's only round three, but Joe looks winded."

"Joe, keep Pastor from dancing!" I shout.

"Back him into a corner, Joe!" Otis say.

Otis and I know what Joe needs.

I say, "Don't let Pastor run you around like that! *Uh-uh* — don't follow him!"

I can't help it no more. I'm up. On my feet, bobbing.

Otis calls out at the radio. "Make *him* come to *you!*"

When I pivot, I see light from the hall get dim at the doorway. Somebody's standing there, watching. It ain't Lila this time, coming to warn us to keep quiet.

It's the bleach man!

I still myself quick. But now all of me's got fight fever.

Otis don't see him right off. He too busy telling Joe how to fight.

"Save your jab for when he comes at your face!" is Otis's advice.

When Otis sees I'm stuck to looking at the door of our ward, he looks, too.

The bleach man, he holding a lantern in one hand. He ripping onto the ward. Measuring his steps.

He stops at our pushed-together cots. Lifts the lantern to near his own face. The blue light turns him to shadows, of chin and nostrils and brows.

The fight's in full swing now. The man in the radio is asking the three of us, *"Can the Brown Bomber keep from losing ground here in round five?"*

The bleach man, he so fixed on me and Otis that he don't see Bird slink past his shoes. He got his palm out in front of him like he's waiting for somebody to drop him a dime. When he speaks, he stops each word before he say the next one. "Give. Me. That. Radio."

Otis hugs his Philco tight. Buries hisself under his blanket. The fight is muffled. The commentary tries to push past the blocked speaker holes. We can only hear snatches of how Joe's doing. It don't sound good.

"Louis . . . wasn't ready for this kind of fight . . . still standing, but catching his breath . . ."

My breath needs catching, too. It's stuck somewhere in my gut. I make myself cough to push it out. The bleach man, he comes closer. He shoves our cots apart with his knee. He flings off Otis's bedcovers. Otis is on his haunches, protecting his radio.

I'm seeing Sampson in my mind. I'm feeling hot hominy. I'm burning but pressed to my spot. *Why can't I help my friend?* My voice is stuck. I'm pinned to my own cot from being afraid of a man who's bringing on hurt.

Otis got his head down. He tucked in like a turtle. Stubborn like a turtle, too. His radio's safe under his belly.

The bleach man reaches in at Otis's side and somehow startles Otis enough to pry away the radio.

The fight blazes from the speaker holes.

"*...the bell to end round seven...,*" say the announcer 'fore the bleach man yanks the radio's plug from the wall socket.

He leaves quick, with light from his lantern shining in front of him.

So much gone so fast.

I wonder, *How will we know what happens to Joe?*

I wonder, *Where did Bird get to?*

I wonder, *Why didn't I fight for Otis? Who snatched my voice from me when it was time to shout, No?*

136

Otis stays curled. Even in the dark, I can see his body trembling. He sniffs into his pillow, flat as a pancake, then starts to whimper, "Daddy…Ma…Daddy… Ma…"

I let Otis be.

I'm fighting again, this time against the stone blocking my throat.

Otis say, "That radio was my promise to Daddy. My hope for Joe."

Otis tells me about how he and his daddy made a deal. Shook on a promise. Put their believing in Joe Louis.

I push my cot back to near Otis's and tell him about me. "I got a daddy and a ma," I whisper. "Still living, not far from here." Then I admit, "I ain't even no real orphan."

I tell Otis about Sampson and his whiskey, and his evil ways.

I tell Otis how my hands got to be twisted nubs of nothing, and how I come to Mercy on a hen truck, and by wishing on Saint Christopher.

I take my medal down from the rafter. I tell Otis about that, too. I tuck Saint Christopher, my protector, into the toe of my sock. Far from the bleach man's reach.

I press my only good finger to my lips.

I say to Otis, "Don't tell Lila none of this."

I say, "Or the bleach man, neither."

Otis lifts his face. His nod shows me he understands.

"Boys!"

Who's rocking my cot?

"Boys, breakfast."

I lift my nose out from under the sheet. No sign of daylight.

I stir. "Ain't hungry."

I squint to find Otis, who's folded hisself tight under his bedcovers. "Me, either," he whines.

Two sure hands lift the foot of my cot and drag me to my right place on the ward. A feeble *meow* peels open the morning.

It's Bird, but where he at?

Another cat cry comes from someplace above us.

Dawn stretches itself through the small window at the way-off end of the ward. More meows, fuller this time, are leaping out from a place I can't see.

I prop onto my elbow. "*Bird*— where you at?"

"*Meeeooooww.*"

My cat is peering down from a crossbeam. I get to my knees, then bring Bird to my lap.

Otis's settled at the foot of my cot. "Bird!"

While the rest of the kids are asleep, we pet our cat.

"You *know* this creature?" Lila asks.

Otis looks at me to answer. "He's a stray," I explain. "I named him Bird, 'cause he's a fighter, like a bird in a box."

Lila says, "He's most definitely been in the ring. Look at those bald patches."

Bird ain't too pleased to see Lila. He's shivering, too.

Lila, she reaches for him, and he throws her a claw. "Well," she say, "this cold makes me irritable, too, though I have more meat on my bones than you do."

Even with him tucked down between my knees, it's easy to see how measly Bird is. "Goodness," Lila say, "this creature is mostly ribs and fur." She tries again to touch Bird, but he's cowering.

"Look at those front paws—two hefty balls of snow." She motions for Bird.

Bird, he slinks back. His gaze is sharp, his eyes stay on Lila. "Here," she say, trying to coax him by putting out both her palms. But he don't want no part of Lila. One paw jabs at her hands, followed real fast by his second ball of snow.

Lila eases away. "Suit yourself, then."

Bird sends out a scrawny meow. Lila say, "Yes, it *is*

time for breakfast, but I'm afraid I can't serve it to you in bed. There's no room service at Mercy. This is not the Waldorf-Astoria Hotel. And you must be an orphan to reside here."

Otis's eyes cut to mine.

"*Are* you an orphan?" Lila asks Bird.

The cat answers with a sure meow.

"No wonder you look so unkempt," Lila say. "A decent mother would not let her child get so bedraggled."

Lila leaves the ward but comes back quick with a pan of milk she sets between us.

That cat, he's stymied. His tiny pink tongue licks at his chops. He's scared, and eager, too.

"It's *okay,*" Otis say.

"Come," Lila say. "I made this special from a can of Mayflower condensed and water."

This cat sure is stubborn. Won't budge.

"We insist on nourishing the children here," Lila tells Bird. "You must stick by the rules, or else Mercy is not the place for you," she says.

"We can't put him out," Otis pleads. "It's cold, and he has no place to go."

I can tell by Lila's smile that she's kidding with the cat. I go along.

"He ain't got no ma or a pa," I say, backing up Otis.

Lila say, "All orphans are welcome here. Even furry ones who don't follow rules, I suppose." She slides closer to Bird. He's getting to poke at the milk with his nose. He licks at it, but slow. "I hope you like Mayflower condensed," Lila say.

"What about the bleach man?" asks Otis.

"The *who?*"

Otis tells Lila how he nicknamed Mr. Sneed.

"What *about* him?" Lila answers.

"What if he finds out we got a cat living here?" I ask.

Lila say, "Leave Sneed to me." Then, "I'm more concerned about this cat's sour temper. He's a cuss of a creature."

"Not when he knows you," Otis explains.

I set one of my hands near the cat's scruff. "Rub him *here.*"

Before Lila can rest down her palm at Bird's nape, he's going for the pan of Mayflower. Lila never even gets to pet Bird. He's too busy lapping the milk. Too busy purring.

HiBERNiA

IF I WERE A SNOWFLAKE, I'D BE SMILING.
But there is not a soul who will call me *Happy* Hibernia on what has to be the coldest morning ever. It is still black dawn, and even my bones are frozen.

I am *Not*-Happy Hibernia.

I *hate* going for rations in winter, especially when the first snow of the season takes me by surprise. And I'm still not over being rained on last October, and missing my chance to audition for Smooth Teddy Wilson. That is a bad memory, stuck on me like the glue on a jelly jar label.

When I am famous, and richer than Madam C. J.

Walker ever was, the only walking I will have to do will be from my house on Easy Street to my butter-colored Bentley parked out front on my driveway paved with glitter.

I sure hope Easy Street shows up soon. My coat is tattered at the hem, and is a flap door for my knees. I have mended this coat so many times that even the sturdiest thread can't hold fabric so tattered.

Sister Wind is whipping hard, sending a chill to my bloomers even. There is no mercy for the gristle on my bones. If I could hurry up, I would. But the snowy streets make for slow going and icicle toes.

Come on, *wagon!*

I'm not pulling this time, I'm bent over, and pushing my wagon from its behind. Sister Wind is now playing my fingers like piano keys. She's pressing hard on my pinkies and thumbs and all the other fingers in between, and blowing a mean rhythm right in my face. My cheeks have never had it so bad. Same for my nose, which is a faucet turned full on. My handkerchief is buried too deep for wiping off nose-run, so I don't bother stopping.

Just keep pushing. And that's what I do until I see the central pavilion up ahead.

As soon as Mr. Haskell's relief truck comes into view, I stop.

The rations line is longer than I have ever seen it, even with the sun only starting to pierce the horizon. Sister Wind has slowed her roll, so I go back to pushing my wagon.

When I reach what I think is the end of the line, I park and settle myself in my wagon's well. I dig for my handkerchief. It takes some fishing, but I finally get to it, forced into the ankle of my sock where I'd shoved it way down so it wouldn't get lost on the way.

I waste no time mopping the place above my lip where my nose faucet's dripped.

"Thankie, Hankie," I murmur.

My handkerchief at least brings a little warmth to *Not*-Happy Hibernia.

Somehow wiping my nose makes me see better. When I lean out the side of my wagon to count the heads in front of me, I spot the sign, big as blazes, propped at the tailgate of the rations truck.

YOUNG PEOPLE SING FOR JOE!
JOIN THE BROWN BOMBER BOX
CAMPAIGN
ALL IT TAKES IS A VOICE AND A DREAM

RAISE BIG $$$ TO WIN
AGES 12 TO 18
FIRST COME, FIRST SERVED

There is practically nothing that could ever make me leave my wagon, but when five special words—*Sing, Voice, Dream, Win,* and *Big*—wave at me with both hands and jump up like new friends ready to say hello, my wagon takes a fast backseat to anything else. Not to mention those dollar signs, which are pretty chorus dancers doing high kicks right next to *Big*.

Now, I know I'm supposed to be good and right and all the rest. But my butter-colored Bentley is waiting, and Easy Street is where I want to be. So I leave my wagon where it is and get out of line.

I rush past everybody else who's waiting. I pretend to have lost my mama, which is really not faking anything, because even though my mama is nowhere near this coldest day ever, I truly *don't* know where my mother is.

That makes it true. *I've lost my mama.*

Somebody shouts, "Hey, you girl, wait your turn like the rest of us!" and all I have to do is whine, "*Mama.* Have you seen my *mama?*"

I try to look a little lost. And confused. And—*Thankie, Hankie!*—I dab at my eyes.

"Maaaama!"

I don't look over one shoulder or the other, and definitely not behind. My sights are on that sign, and I'm *moving*.

"Has anybody seen my mama?"

When I get to the front, Mr. Haskell is glad to see me. "Hibernia, what took you so long? I thought you'd be *first* in line."

"First for *what*?" I'm back to mopping my nose with Thankie Hankie.

"I told your daddy last week after church, and I was sure he'd tell you."

Thankie Hankie's doing double time, and I'm shaking my head. "If this has anything to do with singing, the Reverend C. Elias Tyson has *not* told me."

The people in line are growing restless. "Move it on, child. It's cold out here!"

Thankie Hankie goes back to my alligator tears. *"Maaaama. Where's my maaaama?"*

Mr. Haskell talks fast. "Mike Jacobs, Joe Louis's fight promoter, is sponsoring a young people's campaign in towns all over. It's also a singing contest. They're raising money for Joe Louis—to keep him on the road and in the ring—in the hopes that the Brown Bomber will become the next heavyweight boxing champion of the world."

I'm eager to hear more. I point to the place on the sign that's still waving and dancing in front of me. I ask, "What's 'ALL IT TAKES IS A VOICE AND A DREAM—RAISE BIG \$\$\$ TO WIN' mean?"

"The best singer will earn the most for Joe. Folks plunk down their money in a brown box during the contest. The winner doesn't get the cash. That goes to Joe's campaign. But there will be young singers from everywhere in the state, performing for hundreds of people. This is Mike's way of gathering young fans for Joe Louis."

Now the words on the sign are dancing the Kangaroo. "How will Mike Jacobs know who the *best* singer is?"

Mr. Haskell explains, "It's done by a vote of everyone who comes to the campaign contest. The crowd, by stuffing the Brown Bomber campaign boxes with spare change, names the winner. The child whose box fills with the most money will be the champ." He tells me, "The campaign will happen here in May."

"Well all right, then," I say. "I have time to practice."

I march back to where I think my wagon waits. The line has moved some, so I don't know the spot for sure. I look and look.

No wagon.

I'm forced to turn my searching into the truth. *"My waaagon! Has anybody seen my waaagon?"*

I spend much of the morning walking the fairgrounds, wiping my nose, begging Sister Wind to quit, and calling for my wagon.

I finally give up when I realize I have been gone too long. On my way home, I'm empty-handed. I'm not *pushing* or *pulling* anything. I'm also showing up near to lunchtime with no food rations, no wagon, and no good excuse.

Still, things don't seem so cold. The trees are all shimmery and there are sugarcoated cars parked along the avenue. I'm working hard on what I will tell the reverend. Why am I always the victim of such temptation?

If I'm going to sing in the Brown Bomber Box Campaign, it will mean sneaking past the reverend, which is no fun.

I find a little bit of *Happy* Hibernia, though, when I get to thinking, *Someday my butter-colored Bentley will sure look good in a lace coat of snow.*

I don't tell the reverend about the wagon right away. He finds me dusting Speaky, and he assumes I've put the rations in the larder, which I always do as soon as I return from the fairgrounds.

Later, when the reverend tells me he's preparing for Sunday's sermon in the vestry, I have no doubt he's really sneaking off to listen to his radio. By now I know the routine. Sermons do not get written in the vestry on fight nights.

Sure enough, on the other side of the reverend's sermon room door, I hear Speaky. Tonight there's a boxing match charging from the radio. The reverend is talking to that little wooden box like he's got front-row seats to the ring.

His voice is full of heat. "Bad Boy Johnston planned it this way. He wanted to mess up Joe's knockout record!"

The reverend is agitated. Hearing him holler makes *me* the same way—bothered.

Tonight I don't even need to put my ear to the door. The reverend is talking right out loud. He even turns up the radio's volume.

"Ladies and gentlemen, this has been a night to remember

in the history of Joe Louis's boxing career. Here in round ten, the Brown Bomber, king of the knockout, is named the winner against Bob Pastor. This is the first fight in nearly two years in which Joe Louis has not knocked out his opponent. Even though the Brown Bomber has won the decision, he's come out of this fight looking bad."

I press myself against the door and listen doubly hard.

"The Brown Bomber is tired and panting like a thirsty man in a heat wave. Bob Pastor refused to be knocked down — he's taken some of the shine off Joe Louis's KO glory."

The legs on the reverend's chair creak, then I feel the weight of him pacing the floorboards. My own feet want to take on the floor, and I'm getting pulled in by that messing-up-my-Savoy Skip Gibson!

"This fight was an insult to Joe. An affront to his skill," the reverend grumbles. "What a waste of time!"

Now the reverend sounds out of breath, and desperate for something. And even though all I'm doing is standing and listening, I'm breathing hard, too. I'm whisper-repeating after the reverend. *"Waste of time!"*

Right then the reverend flings open the door and sends me tumbling. I'm nose-to-toe with the reverend's shoelaces. It's hard to think fast when you're smelling leather.

The reverend says, "Get up, Bernie. Speak in defense of yourself."

I'm on my feet, smoothing wrinkles from my nightie. I'm all dried up for an excuse this time. My excuse list keeps growing, and I've got to save my energy for the one about the wagon.

What comes out of my mouth surprises us both. "'A thirsty man in a heat wave'—ha! Joe was probably *thirsty* for a real fight, not a Lindy Hop!"

This is the moment I know prayers are truly answered. The reverend is holding back a chuckle. He can't even look at me. He's pressing a bent knuckle to his lip to keep from letting the chuckle go. He can't keep it in. It escapes when he says, "Get in here, child, sit down."

I cross my legs when I sit in the reverend's chair, which has been shoved back from his writing table, close to Speaky. I say, "Well, it's true. Joe Louis most likely wanted to show his stuff, not prance around. I know how it feels to want to display your talents."

The reverend is leaning against the table's corner. "Oh, do you now," he says.

I cup both hands over my crossed knees. "How's your sermon coming?"

The reverend is sure not chuckling now. He says, "Eavesdropping is a form of deceit, Bernie."

The Lord of letting the right stuff come out of my mouth is with me tonight. I say, "You had the radio turned way up. That's not *eavesdropping,* it's *overhearing*. Besides, I only *overheard* the end, when the commentator said Joe won the fight by a decision."

The reverend shakes his head. His knuckle is back at his lip. That chuckle is threatening him again. "Just like your mama," he says. "She could soften any dereliction, and melt me at the same time. That was Pauline's way. She was clever. Even when she sang in the choir, she would spice up any harmony and turn a hymn into something that was more suited to a nightclub."

"My mother sang in a church choir?"

The reverend nods. "She was a singer in the choir over at the Star of Hope Church in Ithaca. That's where I met her. I often traveled to Star to hear the minister, Reverend Colson Diggs. He was a fine preacher. I wanted to be just like him."

I say my question a second time, more like a truth, not like I'm asking. And when I speak the words, they make me warm. *"Mama sang in a church choir."*

"She had the prettiest voice of them all, Bernie. Sweet as candy."

This talk about my mother makes me call the reverend something I hardly *ever* call him. Something that doesn't come natural. But tonight I just say it, and it sounds right. "Daddy," I say, "Daddy, please, tell me more about Mama. What was her favorite color?"

The reverend, my daddy, gets quiet.

"Pink," he says. "Your mama loved pink. Not that soft pink, either. She liked a color she called *deep-fried* pink."

I scoot my chair closer to my daddy. I don't want to miss a word he's saying.

"What was Mama's favorite food?"

This time Daddy answers fast. It's an easy question for him. "Taffy."

"What did she like to *do* most of all?"

Daddy answers this one quickly, too. He looks sad when he speaks, though. "Sing," he says. "She loved to sing, Bernie. But there was more to it than just that. Your mama sang like her favorite color — deep-fried.

She had a voice that was too hot for the Star of Hope Church." Daddy sighs. "Pauline had sizzling dreams, too. Dreams I couldn't make come true. She wanted a fast, glittery, hot life, far away from here. Far away from me."

Daddy pinches the bridge of his nose.

"Far away from *me*?" I ask.

Silence falls hard.

Daddy doesn't answer right away. When he *does* speak, the words come slowly. "Your mother may be far from you, Bernie, but she left you two very special things — her love for singing, and the voice of an angel."

Then Daddy does something that startles me. He folds me in his weighty arms. He holds me a whole long time, and rests his chin on the top of my head. Daddy is strong, but there is so much gentleness in the way he's hugging me.

Next thing I know, I've got my arms around Daddy's middle. I'm squeezing him with all I've got. "Is she ever coming back?" I ask. My heart is a sand timer, the top filled with hope that's sifting down slowly.

Daddy holds me out in front of him. He looks at me square. "No, Bernie Lee. No. Your mother is off chasing a dream. She was clear when she left that Elmira would never see her again."

That sand timer drains fast now. My hope is disappearing, speeding to the bottom.

Daddy says, "It is a shame she's gone, but I pray every day that she finds whatever it is she's looking for."

"I know about having a dream," I say. "And I understand how Mama could chase after the dream she wants."

Then I admit something I didn't even know was there. "But some of me is angry, too. Mad at Mama for just *leaving*."

I ask Daddy, "Are *you* mad at her for going off the way she did?"

Daddy's thinking, carefully picking the words he wants to say to me. "Bernie, I stayed angry for a long time. Mad at Pauline for what she did by depriving our child of the guidance of a mother."

He rests his palms on both my shoulders. "But I'm not angry at Pauline for who she is. Over time, the mad feelings I've had have passed like a slow-moving dark cloud."

I'm listening to Daddy in the same way his parishioners pay close attention to what he says. I don't want to miss a word. "Whenever I get to thinking about Pauline, all I have to do is look at you. She left so much of herself here by leaving you with me. How can I stay angry at someone who's given me such a special gift?"

"Daddy," I want to know, "how come you wouldn't tell me about Mama before now?"

"I was trying to push her away, Bernie, working to push away my missing her. But as hard as I try, my memories won't leave me alone, especially as you get older and grow to be more like your mother."

I go back to hugging Daddy. "Where'd Mama get the nickname *Praline?*"

Daddy blinks. There's a question in his eyes, then, suddenly, knowing.

I tell him about the picture I found in his Bible, and how I've been keeping my mama with me by sleeping with her picture under my pillow.

Daddy doesn't get mad when he hears this. All he says is "I called your mother Praline because she liked taffy so much, and because her singing was so sweet. And calling her Praline was my own special way of playing with her name, Pauline." There's a happy memory in Daddy's eyes.

Daddy says, "The name Praline stuck. When she

left, she even took that special name with her. She called herself Praline Supreme. That was going to be her show-business name."

"Where's Praline Supreme now?"

"I don't know, Bernie," Daddy says softly.

There they go. The last grains of my heart's hope-sand. Gone.

More quiet settles between Daddy and me.

Daddy fiddles with the dial on his radio. He finds *Swing Time at the Savoy.* We listen together.

I tell Daddy about my lost wagon, and about the Brown Bomber Box Campaign. I don't have to ask him why he didn't tell me about a chance to sing on the radio. That's a question I already know how to answer.

I'm super ready with a list of good reasons why Daddy should let me sing for Joe Louis. I've got at least ten strong arguments. Before I can even pull reason number one out from my pocket, Daddy cups my cheeks in both his hands.

By the look of his eye-on-me stare, I know he's about to give me an order. I'm ready to get scolded about the wagon. Daddy's words are firm. "You are to go back to that fairground."

I nod.

"You are to be the first in line."

I nod twice.

"You are to *sing*."

Five nods fast. "For Joe," I say.

"For you," says my daddy.

OTiS

"WILLIE, LET'S GET BACK AT THE BLEACH man."

"How?"

"Beat him at his own game."

"What game?"

"The game of taking things that don't belong to you."

I motion for Willie to follow me. "Shhh—walk quiet."

We make our way up a set of back stairs that lead from Mercy's kitchen to a place we're not ever, ever allowed to go—to the bleach man's room and privy, where he's got his own bathtub.

I once went into that tiny room when Lila sent me to collect the bleach man's dirty towels for washing. Lila told me then that the bleach man takes his bath on Saturday evenings, eight o'clock.

When we get to the top of the stairs, we hear him. The sound of water being wrung from a washrag is our clue. He's whistling, and swishing water, seems like. Lila was right. Saturday-night bath for the bleach man.

First thing I do is open two of the four windows in the bleach man's room. January at night is colder than a special delivery from the iceman.

Willie starts to understand. He slides open the other two windows, using the heels of his hands.

Outside the privy, the bleach man has left his clothes rumpled and set out a robe and worn slippers. He's even peeled the covers back on his bed. He's looking forward to relaxing later.

When I spot his bath towel hung over the knob on our side of the privy door, I know luck has smiled on us.

The room is as still as a cellar. There's splishy sounds coming from the privy. That's the only noise. Willie and me have to work to be as quiet.

Now, here's the hardest part.

The door to the privy is open a crack. I raise both palms to tell Willie, *stay*. On my belly, I slide to near the privy door, where first I get the towel from the knob.

I gather up the rumpled clothes and bathrobe, and the slippers, too, and shimmy backward toward where Willie's by a window.

I've raised myself onto my haunches, then I'm standing. With one hurl, those clothes and robe and slippers and towel are out the window, into January-at-night.

Even Willie can't fully believe it. I have never seen his eyes go wide, but they're sure open big now, and he's nodding his head — *Yes!*

I point to the bed.

Willie shrugs — *Huh?* — and just watches me, is all.

I'm gathering up the bedcovers and sheets into a bundle that fills both my arms.

Then I chuck 'em.

They're flapping ghosts, taking off into the windy cold.

January-at-night has never had so much fun.

But I'm hardly done.

Black skies look good with puff clouds floating around them.

Bye-bye, bed pillows.

Willie struggles to hold back hard laughing.

Before we can go for more, we hear the gurgle of water being drained from the tub. The bleach man's still whistling, and fumbling to his feet, sounds like.

We are out of there quick and quiet. Like ghosts ourselves.

Getting back at the bleach man isn't funny without witnessing the getting-back.

We're on the other side of the room door, low down, and peeking where we've got the door partway open, just big enough for our four eyes to see in.

When the bleach man comes out, his whistling turns sharp, then stops. January-at-night has snatched him up. The bleach man's confused — and *cold*. He starts to dart, buck naked! Then he's dancing like a chicken, his legs bending every which way.

He can't make sense of it. He hasn't figured out there's a joke on him. I have never seen bleach run so fast!

This is getting back.

So that we don't creak the stairs with our feet, we scurry, facedown, bellies pressed to the steps.

Once we're on our cots in the ward, I give Willie a riddle.

"What do you call a dance that makes you naked and keeps you stepping?"

Willie doesn't even try to answer. He's too busy letting his laugh free.

I tell him, "A *high-knee!*"

SEVEN

EGG TREE

March 1937

WiLLiE

IN BOXING YOU DON'T NEVER KNOW what's coming till it's in your face. You can block, strike, take the punch, or roll with the blow.

When I see Lila on her way up the road, I don't truly know what's coming. She's a round shape in the middle of this spring day. She greets me at the edge of the grass where Mercy meets the road. Lila, she holding a basket filled with apples and wearing a hat with a small brim to cover her face from the sun. It's a man's hat, for fishing, maybe. Ain't nothin' ladylike about it, that hat. *Uh-uh,* nothin' pretty about Lila's droopy hat. She lifts the brim back from her face to wipe her forehead, all dotty with freckles.

Lila's glad to see me. "Apple, Willie?"

She takes quick notice of my hands. I swear, every time Lila looks at these stumps, she does it with eyes that know. "Who wronged you, Willie?" Her asking is sudden but soft.

Something about Lila's straight way of talking makes me just answer, "My pa."

Lila shakes her head. "Some children are better *off* orphaned," she says.

I lean closer to the basket. If I didn't know better, I'd swear them apples was winking at me. They sure do look good. Lila makes one of her apples shine even brighter by buffing it on her sleeve. Then she hands the shining red ball over to me. "Sweetest fruit you'll ever eat," she say.

That's when I see, two of Lila's fingers are bowed. I ain't never looked at Lila's hands close on. Those is some ugly knuckles.

I don't say nothing right off. I cup the apple. It's warm from sitting out on such a bright day.

Lila sees me looking. "Arthritis," she say. "It's a mean affliction when it clings to the joints."

I ask, "It hurt?"

I'm snatching at the apple with my teeth. It's so crunchy, *so good*.

"What's most painful about it is knowing that I will never be a Rosen's Lotion hand model." Lila say it serious, but this is how she being funny.

Lila runs her bent fingers 'long her hat brim.

"I had a no-good daddy," she say real plain. "He was prone to consumption, and often came home tight from moonshine, mad as a hornet."

Anger's putting heat into my cheeks. "My pa was hooked on whiskey, too." I tell Lila about the night Sampson boiled my hands in hot hominy.

She don't look the least bit surprised at what an evil thing it is I'm sharing with her. There's even more knowing in her eyes now. She say, "Liquor can turn a decent man into a monster."

I open and close my fingers to really show Lila what Sampson's done.

She do the same with her arthritis hands. Open, close.

"You want to know how to help your hands, Willie? How to *heal* them?"

Every word Lila say lands on me just right. "How?"

"It's in the dirt, Willie," she says. "Go down to near the grass. That's how you'll make your hands strong again."

I let my apple core drop. Lila say things so certain, I

don't even question her. I stoop to my haunches. Look to Lila for what to do next.

"You see all those weeds lining up along the road?"

I shrug. "Uh-huh."

"Start pulling," Lila say. "Stretch that tight skin that's holding on to your fingers. Work it till it hurts."

I squint at the sun.

"And when you get tired, when the skin on your hands feels like it's about to rip open, turn one of those weeds into your no-good daddy's hair, and pull it out by the roots."

She sees me stalling. *This lady's not playing,* I think. It ain't hard for me to imagine pulling Sampson's hair. But I say to Lila, "Yanking weeds'll help my *hands?*"

"It'll heal *more* than that." Lila crunches on a apple.

Do like she says is all I can think next. *Roll with it.*

I start by tugging a single weed, pulling from the top, coming up with a fistful of green.

"You call that *pulling?*" Lila's got her hat cocked back off her face. "*Use* your hands—*work* them." Now she showing me how by snatching a weed in one snap, with roots and even worms trailing from its bottom. "See what I mean?" She shakes dirt from the tangled mess.

I don't ask no more questions. Neither do Lila.

I grab two weeds at a time. My fingers is right at the

dirt that's biting hard on their roots. Me and those weeds, we playing a mean tug-of-war, and I want to win.

I give them weeds all I got—pull, pull, *pull*. My hands—*uh*—they throbbing as I jerk up them stubborn plants. The skin on my knuckles is a tight glove. Keeps my fingers from bending all the way. But I ain't stopping. *Uh-uh,* won't quit.

What Lila's got coming is now right in my face.

"There are no rules," Lila say. "Only that you *go at it*."

I throw each weed behind me, working my way forward, along the road on my knees.

Pull. Toss. *Pull. Toss. Pull.*

I got a whole rhythm going. It's the rhythm of the peanut bag, clanging from its iron link—*1-1-2-2-1-1-2-2!*

It's the beat of my fists slamming the body bag—*Bam! Bam! Bam!*—while my heart and nerves and muscles and breath fight to keep going.

The scar from where Bird sunk his claw, it's now a raw red line along my thumb. Boy, does it sting from being strained against itself.

"Tired?" Lila asks.

"Naw," I say, swallowing the road dust that flies at my face.

"How do your hands feel?" Lila asks.

"Stronger," I say.

"How about the rest of you?"

I blow a quick breath.

"Stronger still."

Next morning, Lila, she surprises me again. Not with weeds, but with a tree. She gone and climbed to the top of Mercy's tallest oak. I'm on the side porch, looking straight up.

"Mrs. Weiss, come down from there! You'll break your neck! What on earth are you doing?"

"I'm not *on* earth, Mr. Sneed. I am in a tree."

"I can see you're *in* a tree, Mrs. Weiss. Have you lost your mind?"

"No, Mr. Sneed, I have not lost my mind. But I can't seem to locate the twine I brought with me. Do you see a ball of string down there?"

"Mrs. Weiss, I order you to come down this instant! I am responsible for your welfare while you are on the premises of this facility. What has led you to — to — climb a tree?"

"I'm decorating."

"Decorating?"

"Have you not heard of an egg tree, Mr. Sneed? It is the proper way to announce the coming of Easter."

"Have you gone mad, woman?"

"Lack of joy is the first sign of madness, Mr. Sneed. As an Easter greeting to all who pass our property, I'm hanging eggs from the branches of Mercy's biggest tree. Eggs that I've dyed with beet juice and carrot pulp. This brings me great joy. I am not a madwoman."

"Mrs. Weiss, the Mercy Home for Negro Orphans is not a popular passing spot. Not many people will see the eggs. Please, I urge you, come *down*."

Much as I don't like the bleach man, I wish Lila'd come out of that tree. I wouldn't climb that high up myself, even. I wonder if Lila's touched in the head. *She crazy?* I wonder.

"Mr. Sneed, look there, right by your foot! I see the twine! It must have fallen from my apron while I was climbing. Toss it up to me, will you?"

"I will *not!*"

I start for the twine. I'm eager to help Lila, till she say to the bleach man, "Then you leave me no choice but to make my way down, then climb back up to the top of this tree."

"Mrs. Weiss, this is dangerous. Stay where you are. I'll — I'll — bring the string to you."

"Oh, thank you, Mr. Sneed. That would prevent my eggs from falling. I have taken great care to secure them in the folds of my skirt."

"Here I come, Mrs. Weiss."

More than anything, I wanna run. *Uh-huh,* I gotta find Otis. But *uh-uh,* I sure ain't gonna miss *this.* I stay put. No way I'm moving.

"Oh, my, be careful, Mr. Sneed!"

"Mrs. Weiss, my foot is — it's slipping!"

"Here, grab on to my hem!"

"Mrs. Weiss, your eggs are falling on my head!"

"Goodness gracious, Mr. Sneed. I'm so glad the eggs are hard-boiled. But what a shame. I'm losing some of the brightest ones. Don't let go, though. And put your left foot into the tree fork, where that branch is strongest. Easy... There you go... Now sit back a bit on the limb, right next to me."

I'm giving up worrying about Lila. She don't need my help. It's the bleach man who's the most troubled, and he can forget getting anything from me.

"Mrs. Weiss, so help me, if I become injured, I'll —"

"Mr. Sneed, two of my eggs have managed to land in your shirt pocket! That means I've lost only a few. Thank you, Mr. Sneed. There are plenty of eggs left in my skirt, quite enough to decorate our egg tree. Would you kindly hand me the twine?"

"Mrs. Weiss, you have violated every rule of employment at this establishment. I have no choice but to —"

"You have no choice but to sit on this limb and help me decorate this tree, Mr. Sneed. You are not a very competent climber. If you even *try* to get down on your own, you will no doubt fall. You're stuck with me, Mr. Sneed. In a tree."

"Mrs. Weiss, here is the twine."

"Here is an egg, Mr. Sneed. It is the brightest one I have. Pink, from the beet juice. Now, loop the twine around the egg's middle, and leave a tail long enough for hanging the egg from a branch. Once you have the right size string, I'll cut the end from the ball of twine. I've brought my late husband's army knife."

"Like — like this?"

"Perfect."

"Mrs. Weiss, you have me under duress! Pass me an orange egg. I'll hang that one next."

"Certainly, Mr. Sneed. Two eggs. On a limb. Side by side. Very festive."

I race inside. "Otis, come see!"

HiBERNiA

IT SEEMS MRS. TRASK, OUR CHURCH AC-
companist, has a beetle stuck under her wig. She is all
full of agitation, and I'm sure not helping matters.

We're not even two bars into "I'm Gonna Sing"
when Mrs. Trask pulls her fingers back from the piano
keys and stops playing. She stands up sharply from the
piano bench, both hands at her hips. "Who's turning
our hymn into a juke-joint rag?" she wants to know.

One at a time, she gives each and every one of us in
the True Vine Baptist Youth Singers a hard stare.
"This is a rehearsal for a *church* choir, not an audition
for a honky-tonk."

Nobody says anything. When Mrs. Trask's stare

lands on me, I take quick little bites from my thumbnail. I don't let my eyes meet hers. I do a good job of inspecting the place where Daddy's just fixed a leak in the ceiling.

Most times I hate being in the choir's back line, but that's what you get when you're all legs and tall as timber. A true star like me deserves front-row treatment. Today, though, I'm grateful to be tucked behind Fay Nims, the second soprano in the front row.

Still, Mrs. Trask has a way of spotting me. She eyes me longer than the other kids.

"Let's begin again," she says. There's suspicion on her face.

When Mrs. Trask hits a G chord to start us off, I keep my voice simple. I get through the whole first verse, singing like any good church soprano should.

> *"I'm gonna sing when the Spirit says sing —*
> *I'm gonna sing when the Spirit says sing —*
> *I'm gonna sing when the Spirit says sing —*
> *And obey the Spirit of the Lord."*

But then, fast on the heels of *obey the Spirit of the Lord* comes the second verse — *I'm gonna shout when the Spirit says shout.*

Something winds up in me, ready to swing. When that D7 chord flies free from those piano keys, I can't help myself.

I'm gonna shout when the Spirit says shoooouuuut turns into a pink-fried tune. I let the *Spirit of the Lord* rise out of me like I'm a Praline Supreme.

Mrs. Trask blows her gasket! She is off that piano bench in a snap. "This is not the home of dance music. This is a church! Which one of you is disrespecting our place of worship?"

Now it isn't just Mrs. Trask who's got her eye on me. Near to half the choir is looking in my direction. Fay Nims is the first to speak. "That jazzifying is coming from Hibernia," she says.

Everybody agrees with Fay. "Yeah," says Robert Pettiford, "Hibernia's putting all kinds of feathers onto our song."

"And she's making *me* want to do it," admits Carla Wright, my church-gossip friend.

My thumb is back at my teeth, getting its nail chewed to the quick. I waste no time explaining myself. "Mrs. Trask, I…I…was so moved by the…the…uh… Spirit of the Lord that I got all carried away. If you play the first verse again, I'll show you how *respectfully* I can deliver the tune."

Mrs. Trask looks at me sideways, but she agrees. She tells the other kids to take a break. They slide into the first-row pew, where they watch me do a straight-as-rain version of "I'm Gonna Sing."

I don't add a single flip. I use my very best diction and pitch. I make my voice go full on the vowels and land hard on the consonants to shape the song perfectly. The Gs and D7s fill every corner of our rickety church.

The other kids, even Fay Nims, clap politely. Mrs. Trask turns around on her bench. "You *do* have a gift, child," she admits. "That rendition is worthy of a solo."

I give a little smile, all humble.

Mrs. Trask says, "Your father has arranged for us to perform another concert — an Easter chorus — for the children at the Mercy Home for Negro Orphans. Together we'll sing a selection of songs fitting for the spring season. Hibernia, you alone can perform 'I'm Gonna Sing.'"

I try to look bashful about the whole thing. "Oh, Mrs. Trask," I say, "thank you. I'll sing properly. For the orphans."

Mrs. Trask ends our rehearsal by collecting her sheet music and asking us to make sure we take our belongings with us when we leave. As soon as Mrs. Trask is gone, I gather the other singers near the piano. I work on Carla Wright first. "You know what, Carla? If you feel like you want to do a little jazzifying, we could try it now. What can it hurt? We're just messin' around."

I take Mrs. Trask's place at the piano bench. I strike a G chord and start off like thunder. Forget the first verse. I go right to the part about shouting.

"I'm gonna shout when the Spirit says a-shoooouuuut!

I'm gonna shout when the Spirit says a-shoooouuuut!

I'm gonna shout when the Spirit says a-shoooouuuut!"

Carla latches on to the tempo. She rides the rhythm all the way. She does something you're never, ever supposed to do in the Lord's house—she snaps her fingers.

Fay Nims is jazzifying like True Vine Baptist is the Apollo Theater in Harlem. And Robert Pettiford, hoo-boy, he is bringing it all together with a gutbucket bass. Soon every kid in the choir has picked up on the jam. My fingers, sawed-off nails and all, have a mind of their own. They are doing a Lindy Hop all over the piano keyboard.

Our little church is swelling with something wonderful.

> *"I'm gonna shout when the Spirit says a-shoooouuuut!*
> *I'm gonna shout when the Spirit says a-shoooouuuut!*
> *I'm gonna shout when the Spirit says a-shoooouuuut!*
> *And obeeeyyy the Spirit of the Looorrrrd!"*

After all the verses — after *preaching* when the spirit says *a-preach,* and *praying* when the spirit says *a-pray,* and *singing* when the spirit says *a-siiiing* — we are all giddy and laughing, and feeling fine.

I say, "Those orphan kids could probably use a little Easter jazzifying. How about we show them the way we've worked our song?"

Fay goes back to thinking like a tattletale. "Mrs. Trask will have our heads."

I say, "Mrs. Trask objects to letting loose here in *church*. She didn't say anything about how you're supposed to sing in an orphanage."

Carla agrees with me. "Easter *is* a time for rejoicing."

Robert Pettiford is still humming. He only stops to add his two cents. "I sure sounded good, didn't I?"

It doesn't take too much arm-twisting before everyone, even Fay Nims, agrees that we'll give the kids at the Mercy Home for Negro Orphans an Easter concert they won't ever forget.

The best part is the pink-fried rendition of "I'm Gonna Sing," with Hibernia Lee Tyson doing a sizzling solo way out front.

OTiS

THE FIRST VISITS ME FAINT AS A WHISPER.

Why do gingerbread men wear long pants?

That's the funniest one ever. Funny like when hard tickling doesn't stop.

The riddle's hurling out from the radio. My Philco is telling me Daddy's riddle-jokes. Louder comes the next one, a blast from the Philco's speaker.

How do you stop a snake from striking?

The radio's so noisy, with people from inside the Philco giggling and clapping about the riddle.

I'm laughing so hard, I'm crying.

And heaving.

And struggling to find my breath.

And grabbing on to the Philco, hugging it to my chest where pounding strikes fast.

At first, this laughing won't let me free. But somehow it spins itself backward, releases me, drops me down a hole. Now I'm crying so hard, I'm *crying*.

The Philco's volume turns up, up. Radio voices thump at the place where the speaker is pressed to me, full blast from the Philco. I'm clinging on to the sound.

Don't let it go. Shake on a promise. Hope.

I'm feetfirst, still on my way to some below place. My legs are flailing to find anything that will let me stand. I'm blinking into the darkness of Ma and Daddy gone. I can't see anything but the wide-open black of being sad. Of missing my folks, and wanting them, is all.

The riddles repeat:

Why do gingerbread men wear long pants?

How do you stop a snake from striking?

They wake me from a solid sleep as they shout to greet me. They're curling in at the edges of my mind, slamming like an angry storm.

These are Daddy's riddle-jokes that made Ma and me roll ourselves silly.

When I listen even harder, I hear Daddy's voice — and Daddy's grinding laugh, and Ma's giggle — winding themselves through the riddles.

I'm partway asleep, partway awake. The riddles poke at me, same as a woodpecker does to a tree. Those riddles are doing double time.

I call out their answers just as fast.

"Because they have crummy legs!"

"Pay it a decent wage!"

I've smacked onto a bed of hay. I try to lower the radio's sound, but it's no use. So I shake it, hard as I can. The Philco sputters until it's almost quiet.

More riddles:

Why did the green tomato turn red?

What do whales eat?

Then softness comes. The warmth of a palm on my forehead helps me toward wakefulness. At first, my partway sleeping mind is showing me Ma's gentle hands. My partway sleeping mind is telling me I feel Ma's hands, too.

I call for her. "Ma, Ma…"

Lila's voice brings me fully awake. "Otis…Otis, honey, you were having a nightmare. You were talking in your sleep."

Lila is holding a cup of water. "Sit up for a moment, drink this."

It's hard to open my eyes. My lids are heavy hoods trying to keep me sleeping. I manage to sip some water, but the water dribbles down my front. I'm holding tight to my pillow, which is sweaty from my pressing on it. It had been the Philco in my dream.

"Easy now," Lila says, folding my flat pillow to prop behind me.

Partway sleeping, I say, "Lila, why did the green tomato turn red?"

Lila looks puzzled, but like she's trying to understand, too. "Settle down, now," she says gently. "Have more water. It's nice and cold."

My partway sleeping mind is leaving me. The heavy lids are lifting back from my eyes. I tell Lila, "The riddle about the green tomato was one of my daddy's most favorites. My pa was so good at making up riddles. He could stump most people, but make them laugh, too."

Lila tries to answer, but she acts like she's playing along with something, not really knowing I mean for her to do her best to solve the riddle.

Lila says, "I suppose if I were a green tomato, I'd turn red because I was feeling saucy."

I shake my head. I show Lila how you're supposed to do riddles. "Ask *me* the riddle," I tell her.

"Very good, then," she says. "Why did the green tomato turn red?"

I come back fast with my answer: "Because it saw the salad dressing!"

Lila is just as quick. "Well," she says, "the tomato most likely felt a little saucy after seeing the undressed salad."

I rub the partway sleeping crust from my eyes. I say to Lila, "Try another one. Just answer what you think, right off." I ask her, "Are you ready?"

"Ready."

"What do whales eat?"

Lila taps at the place right under her nose. "Well," she begins, "I suppose if I were a hungry whale—"

"Don't go supposing, Lila. Just *say* something."

Lila's face brightens with figuring on the answer. "Fish and ships."

"Right, Lila, *right*—fish and ships!"

Lila drinks some of the water she's brought for me. "Your daddy must have been a very special man," she says softly.

"So special."

I tell Lila about the crash that took Ma and Daddy. How the hay truck came right at them in our truck's cab but missed me because I was riding on the flatbed, far enough from the flames.

"Goodness, child," she says. "Were you hurt badly?"

"Scratched some. But I was able to run to our church, where people helped me."

My neck goes hot talking about all of this. Being with Lila is so easy, though. Even describing bad things feels safe.

I tell her all about Daddy's Philco.

"When that hay truck was heading toward us, I held on to the Philco tight as I could. It's a good thing, too. Nothing happened to the radio in the crash. That Philco is how I remember Daddy and Ma best. Daddy had given me the radio as a way to remember him when he went to work in Philadelphia, and also for following Joe Louis," I explain.

Then I tell Lila how the bleach man snatched my radio from me.

She is quick to say, "Sneed is a scab!" Her words fling as fast as spit. "I know I shouldn't use such language with you children, but what a *scab,*" she repeats.

She offers a sip more water, and tells me about a special man and *his* radio. Lila's husband's name was Gus. "Pieces of him come to me in my dreams, too," she says.

She tells me that Gus loved Joe Louis, and how Gus died just a few months back.

Then Lila gets lost in a memory. "I remember when I first met Gus. He had always loved the fights."

"My daddy, too," I say.

"Gus could rattle off Joe Louis statistics at the snap of a finger."

Lila starts playing like she's Gus knowing stuff about Joe: "A born slugger, called the Brown Bomber because of his killer punches."

Now I do like I'm Daddy, knowing about Joe, too: "The boy turned pro at age twenty."

Lila smiles at our Be-Gus, Be-Daddy game. She says, "And how many times did Gus remind me, 'About a year and a half ago in New York, Joe knocked out Max Baer in the fourth round'?"

"And," I say, being Daddy, "'In Chicago, Joe KO'd Charley Retzlaff in round *one*. Poor Charley didn't know what hit him.'"

Lila says, "Once Gus got started, it was hard to stop him. There were many nights I let him whirl, just for the fun of seeing him go on so much about Joe."

"Same with Daddy," I say.

Lila sighs. "Gus died happily, I suppose, doing something that brought him joy." Softly she says, "I sure loved him."

I whisper, "Lila, *I* got a love."

I show Lila my paper chain. "I made it from Chewsy Time wrappers. From gum my pa brought me once."

Lila gently runs her fingers across the chain links. "Otis, this is beautiful."

"Willie helped me make it. It's a present for a girl at the True Vine Baptist Church, one of the singers who came to Mercy at Christmastime."

Lila nods. She knows who I mean. "Hibernia, the reverend's daughter."

"Hibernia." Just saying it makes behind my ears go warm.

"Is that why you were asking about presents and girls and such?"

I answer with a question. "You go to True Vine Baptist, right?"

Lila nods.

"Would you give Hibernia the chain? Would you tell her it's from me, and that I made it for her?"

"Why don't *you* give it to her?"

I explain how when we went to True Vine, I messed up on the riddle, and Hibernia called me a goof-head. And said my feet are goofy, too. And how I was so much paying attention to the Plan of the Three S's that I forgot to introduce myself.

"I see," Lila says, is all.

She carefully coils the chain, tucks it into her apron pocket. "Consider it done."

"Tell Hibernia my name," I insist. "Say it's from Otis."

Lila thumbs my chin. "I'll tell her it's from someone very special."

EIGHT

DAFFODILS

April 1937

HiBERNiA

"GREASE ME, SPEAKY!"

I don't care if everybody in Elmira hears me talking to Daddy's radio. Let them say whatever they want about Hibernia Lee Tyson. They'll need to remember my name, *anyway,* when news spreads that it was me whose singing in the Brown Bomber Box Campaign earned enough to fill an entire box with plenty of money to help Joe Louis get to his big fight.

I'm supposed to be *cleaning* Speaky, not *conversating* with him. But I've hit on a way to dust and also rehearse for the Brown Bomber Box Campaign at the same time. All I have to do is make friends with the radio by talking *to* it, and singing *with* it, and allowing us to each do what we do best — let our tunes fly.

Housework goes faster when you sing. With Daddy out on prayer calls for the afternoon, Speaky and me can really *go*. That's why I'm happy to dust Daddy's radio. It's a piece of cake when you invite the CBS Radio Network to the party. "Hey, Speaky, let's swing!"

I waste no time getting to the station, where sounds from the Savoy Ballroom bring the Chick Webb Orchestra into the vestry. I don't even have to fiddle too much with the tuning knob. I ease past radio static and comedy programs and come right to the spot where "Harlem Congo" flares as hot as bootleg Tabasco. Chick Webb and his band are bringing it home. And, oh, can Chick *slam*.

He doesn't *play* his drums, he *works* them.

When the radio announcer invites his listeners to sing, I'm there, *Happy* Hibernia. Not singing, but *siiinging*.

Working the downbeat.

Milking the backbeat.

Siiinging like tomorrow won't ever come.

My dust rag makes the best dance partner there is

'cause the rag lets me lead. I shimmy the rag, then land it with a swift rhythm —*slap!*—onto Speaky's head. I polish till the radio's wood is slick. "Gleam *on,* Speaky, gleam *on!*"

Here comes Chick's drum solo—hitting hard!

His timpani sets "Harlem Congo"—and Hibernia Lee Tyson—on fire.

As far as cleaning goes, the dust-rag flip is my specialty. I fling the rag from behind my back, wrist-snap it once, hard, and put a shine on Speaky's wood-tone side. The whole time I'm *siiinging.*

Busting loose in the sermon room.

Showing my dust rag who's boss.

Fierce Bernie Lee.

That's me.

I wish Joe Louis knew how lucky he was to have Hibernia *siiinging* for his campaign. Thanks to me, Joe's promoter will be able to dress him like a king for his big fight. He'll look good in the ring.

Now I'm really rehearsing, putting my all into the song. Those fairgrounds spread out far, and I want to make sure everybody and everybody's cousin can hear me. Even Mrs. Trask from church says the best way to deliver a song is to *project.* And the best way to *impress* while you're *projecting* is to smile. Because part of winning is grinning.

So I snap my rag, *siiiing* with Chick and his orchestra, and *project* loud enough to shoo the sparrows off our roof.

When a knock comes to the door, there's enough force behind it to stop my song.

"Hello, hello!" a voice calls.

Now I'm *Not*-Happy Hibernia because my *siiiinging* has been interrupted.

I turn down the radio, tuck the tail of my rag into my skirt's waistband.

More knocking rattles the screen door. "Good afternoon!"

It's not a voice I recognize, but as soon as I get to the screen door and see the copper-colored hair, I know the face. It's that lady from the Mercy Home for Negro Orphans. She's holding a bunch of daffodils at her chest and clutching a small paper bag. Her dress is the yellow one from Baptism Sunday, the best thing she owns, probably. I can't help but inspect for the doughnut-roll socks. They're gone, thank goodness. Maybe she's put them away for spring. Her shoes are the same, though. Still ugly. Still shaped around her onion bunions.

"May I come in?"

Now, any girl who's got a thimble of sense knows you can't open the door for just anybody who knocks. But, well, she *is* smiling. And she *isn't* just anybody. And those flowers are as bright as the day.

"This'll take only a moment," she says. "I was hoping we could have a word."

She steps closer to the screen door. "These are for you." She holds up the daffodils and the bag. "Gifts to welcome spring, and a belated thank-you for such a rousing holiday concert."

I look closely at what she's brought.

She explains, "The flowers are from me. The gift in the bag is from Otis, one of the boys at Mercy. He made it especially for you, with the help of his friend, Willie, another one of our children."

"Otis," I say, knowing just who she means. "He's the boy with the riddle, right?"

She smiles. "Otis Rollins."

Nobody has ever brought me flowers for singing. I motion for her to step back so I can swing open the door. I take the flowers and the bag and set them down. With all this lady's talking, I forget about them for the moment.

The lady says, "You and I have enjoyed several brief

encounters, but we've never truly been introduced. My name is Lila Weiss."

"I'm Hibernia Lee Tyson."

"I know who *you* are," says Lila Weiss. "And I must ask. Where did you learn to sing with such fortitude?"

"It comes natural, I guess."

"You certainly have a gift," she says.

I giggle. "I do, don't I."

It's then that I start to miss Chick Webb, and realize that he and the Savoy are gone. Now there's some advertisement for tooth powder chiming from the radio. I'm eager for more "Harlem Congo," but what I get instead makes *Not*-Happy Hibernia even more *Not*-Happy. It's Skip Gibson's Boxing Commentary, butting in — again!

That blasted Skip! He must be the president of the Let's Make Hibernia Lee Tyson *Not*-Happy Club.

"Ladies and gents, the date is set. On June the twenty-second the Brown Bomber will go head-to-head with James Braddock for the world heavyweight title. There's bets everywhere about this fight. Louis is the two-to-one favorite. But does he have what it takes to go all the way? Can he unseat the champion?"

"Do you hear that?" Lila Weiss says. "Joe Louis is fighting for the world heavyweight title."

Skip's got Lila's attention, and for once, he's got mine. I'm hoping he'll mention Joe's Brown Bomber Box Campaign. I invite Lila Weiss inside. I'm eager to close the door. Without the screen between us, I start to worry about flies and mosquitoes taking this as their chance to have a bug party in Daddy's sermon room.

Lila goes right to the radio. She fiddles with the knob to sharpen the sound. I guess this lady doesn't ask before touching. She catches herself. "Oh, goodness, excuse me."

I offer her a seat. *Yes, excuse you,* I think. *Onion bunions, and no manners.*

"Hibernia, I am not a woman who gambles or puts much stock in sports and the gossip that comes with it. But there is a rumor circulating about Joe Louis. There is all kinds of speculation and debate about his next match against James Braddock for the heavyweight championship of the world."

Maybe Lila Weiss knows something about Joe's Brown Bomber Box Campaign. But I can't even squeeze in the question. There's a motor driving her mouth. I tug at my dust rag. Lila says, "Some people believe it's a cinch that Joe will win. Others think Joe doesn't stand a chance against Braddock, who is known as one of the toughest fighters anywhere."

Skip continues his commentary. Lila hushes up.

"Louis is laying low until he steps into the ring with Braddock. Mike Jacobs, Louis's promoter, has hired Joe a private railroad car to take him on a western tour of small-potato exhibition matches."

This lady is ready to burst open, the same as the stitching on her shoes is about to give way to her onion bunions. She's *Happy* Lila Weiss.

Now *she's* the one speaking to Speaky. "How do you like that? They're treating Joe like royalty!"

I start in with my question: "Do you know anything about Mike Jacobs's Brown Bomber Box Cam —"

But *Happy* Lila Weiss is getting even *happier*.

She's slowed down some, and is picking her words carefully. "Hibernia, I'm a firm believer in the power of prayer," she begins. "I trust that being the daughter of such a prodigious preacher, and the deliverer of such inspired singing, you share my sentiment."

I shrug. "I guess so."

Happy Lila Weiss says, "I don't like to waste precious

time entertaining hearsay, but I am finding it difficult to keep my mind off this fight. You see, my late husband was an avid follower of boxing—and a huge Joe Louis fan—and more than anything, it would have brought him no greater joy than to see Joe Louis become the heavyweight champ of the world."

Lila's sincere, but she sure can ramble. Finally, she gets to her point. "Hibernia, we need a prayer. A prayer for Joe Louis."

"You want *me* to pray for the Brown Bomber?"

Like Daddy, Lila Weiss must be making prayer calls today.

"Yes, for Joe."

Lila hikes her skirt, and kneels, right in front of Speaky! Her knees are two hams pressed to the floorboards. "Supplication is always best for prayer," she says. She motions for me to kneel with her.

I have been asked to say a lot of prayers in my life, but none like this. "I'll kneel, but my skirt stays where it is," I say.

Lila Weiss bows her head. She shuts both her eyes. Her hands are folded tight.

I've rested the daffodils and brown bag on the small table where Speaky sits. The daffodils' yellow faces watch up at me and this lady with the pork knees.

Happy Lila Weiss lowers her voice. "Hibernia, why don't you start us off."

I'm lost. I know the Lord's Prayer, a Thanksgiving prayer, and even a prayer for sick dogs. But a Joe Louis prayer?

Lila Weiss opens her eyes to look at me sideways. "Just pray what comes to you. Prayer is a petition. All you have to do is petition on Joe's behalf."

She goes back to a lowered head and closed eyes. She is concentrating on whatever it is I'm about to say.

My head is bent, but I've only got one eye shut. My other eye roams the room. Maybe by looking around I'll get some idea about what kind of *petition* I can make for Joe.

Lila Weiss is expecting something special from me, but I'm as empty as an overdrawn bank account. But okay, sometimes performers have to improvise. So I try.

"Lord," my lone eye is still searching for even a speck of inspiration. "Please help Joe Louis to fight with might, and to be all right. And to—"

This is the one time I'm glad that Skip is back with his commentary. Speaky has saved me!

"America is waiting and wondering on the Brown

Bomber. Every radio in our nation will be tuned in to the Louis-Braddock fight. All ears will be listening for boxing's future."

Lila Weiss cuts in. She can't help herself. *She's* the one with the *petition*. This is the easiest prayer I've ever said. *Happy* Lila Weiss is doing all the work.

"Heavenly Father, in all your goodness, bless Joe Louis with your powerful hand. Make him strong. Lead him in the ways of prizefighting."

I'm back to both eyes open. Even as the reverend's daughter, I have never seen so much true feeling behind a prayer.

Lila sighs. "And, dear Lord, let Joe Louis take James Braddock out quickly and with a steady fist. If James Braddock falls in the ring, please give the referee the fitness he needs to count down swiftly. Amen."

"Amen, times ten," I say.

After Lila leaves, I remember the gifts she's brought. I put the daffodils in a jar with water, and set the flowers on our kitchen table, where they greet Daddy when he comes home for supper. I tell Daddy about Lila's visit. He looks pleased.

"Daddy," I ask, "what is *supplication?*"

Daddy's answer is simple. "Humbling yourself."

"What's a *petition?*" I want to know.

"A request from the most sincere heart."

Later, I open the crumpled bag from Lila, reach down in, and pull out something so special that not even Sears, Roebuck sells it.

WiLLiE

Let's go, mighty Joe.
Battle like the Alamo.
Hey, hey, mighty Joe.
Time to bomb 'em — there you go!
Go, go, mighty Joe!
Get 'em good — there you go.

WHERE'S THAT MUSIC COMING FROM?
Muffled and low, singing about Joe Louis. Am I
dreaming about Joe? Is Joe creeping up to me in the
late nighttime?

I listen hard. Here come the refrain.

Hey, hey, mighty Joe.
Time to bomb 'em — there you go!
Go, go, mighty Joe!
Get 'em good — there you go.

This song ain't working up from my dreams. It's from out back. There's static behind the music. The song about Joe is spilling from a radio. Pulling me awake. Gets me humming.

Let's go, mighty Joe.
Battle like the Alamo.

I don't know a thing about no Alamo, but if it has to do with Joe Louis, it must be mighty.

I follow the trail of yellow light being sent into the ward by the bulb hanging from the latrine's ceiling. But it's the music I'm after, not the latrine. It's that refrain — *Hey, hey, mighty Joe. Time to bomb 'em — there you go!* — leading me past the intake table to out back. To Mercy's one plot of grass. To our dumb little yard with a shed for storing food rations.

As I go, the radio's rattly music gets louder. But it's still stifled. Still pressed back from coming in clear. The moon's looking like a fingernail hooked around a bundle of clouds. And them crickets is making their own music. *Uh-huh,* them crickets is singing along for Joe.

Morning must be coming. The skin on my feet is getting a dew bath from the wetness dawn has spread on the grass. I move slow, closer and closer to where I hear the music.

It's the bleach man, leaning against a sack, snoring loud as a roadster. He's got a box of canned peas nearby, only half emptied. I figure he must have been stacking the cans, took a rest, and fell asleep. And there's Otis's radio, cradled like a baby in the crook of the bleach man's arm. He's propped by the corner, where the radio's plugged in. The speaker holes, they're turned in to the bleach man's belly. Joe's song is pressed against the handle of skin where the bleach man's belt is meeting up with his pants.

My mouth makes out what I wish I could say. My words is more quiet than a whisper. "Come on, bleach man, try messing with me now."

I watch the radio rise and fall against the bleach man's body when he breathes. I'm by him enough to see his bottom lip dropped low, catching his drool.

I make-believe I'm Joe Louis. I pretend the bleach man is some sorry sack, ready to fall. From where I stand in the shadow of the moon, I *jab, jab, jab,* at the air in front of the bleach man's face. He ain't nowhere near to waking up. He don't even know he's my fake fight, getting beat to pine pulp.

Get up, you louse! The words is still just my lips shaping 'em. No sound to what I'm saying. *Come to your feet so's I can knock you back down!*

I'm full of power each time I jab into the blue dawn. *Uh-huh.* My fists fly at the twilight around me, and I'm so, so strong. My whole body's churned up. Gets both my punches going.

Jab! Jab! Jab!

I stutter-step, in toward the bleach man, then back. *Think you can take that radio from my friend? Well, take this!*

Now I'm full out fighting. Shoulders heavy into the punches. Elbows and wrists snapping hard when I land one near his face. And my hands—they's fully bent. No more tight skin holding 'em open. No more halfway trying to fold 'em closed. Both hands is all the way rolled tight for punching hard!

Battle like the Alamo...

...Get 'em good—there you go.

Morning drops down like a blanket of butter. I shake my fists free for the final blow. The last of the fight ain't a punch, though.

It's a quiet win.

I move in closer to the bleach man. I'm now back to what Lila showed me about using my hands. What she explained about fighting in a different way.

I carefully lift the radio from the bend in the bleach man's arm. I get the radio more easy than plucking a dandelion.

Now I *am* a champ. *Uh-huh,* this fight's all mine.

When I get to the ward, I start to wake Otis but then think better on it. Instead, I slide the radio onto the edge of Otis's pillow.

"Dream good now," I whisper. "Your Philco's back."

OTiS

THE TRUE VINE BAPTIST YOUTH SINGERS
are here again, bringing us Easter songs. They start
with "Oh, He Has A-Risen," then go on to "Believe in
the New Day."

This time I have set my dayroom chair right close to
where they are. Hibernia's behind the other kids, like
before. And she's singing just as beautifully. But today
she's holding something back, not letting her voice fly
as high.

Then the lady at the piano says, "We will now have
a solo selection sung by Hibernia Lee Tyson."

Willie bumps his shoulder to mine. "Ain't that ya girl?"

"Shhh," I whisper. "She's coming to the front."

Hibernia steps out from the back row. She goes to where the lady at the piano is seated. That's when I see it around her neck. Hibernia Lee Tyson is wearing the gum-wrapper chain woven by me and Willie! She's fastened each end to make a necklace! The wrapper necklace is a pretty strand of colors against her blue collar.

"See that?" Willie says.

I can't even talk. All's I can do is nod.

The lady at the piano strikes a chord. Hibernia takes a breath. She is looking straight at me. She is running her fingers along the gum-wrapper-chain necklace. Then she lets her voice free:

> *"I'm gonna sing when the Spirit says siiiing!*
> *I'm gonna sing when the Spirit says siiiing!*
> *I'm gonna sing when the Spirit says siiiing!*
> *And obey the Spirit of the Lord."*

The first verse is soft and full.

At the next verse, the choir behind Hibernia joins in. Hibernia's singing goes from sweet to sassy. She's put a raspy twist on the song.

"I'm gonna preach when the Spirit says a-preeeaaach!

I'm gonna preach when the Spirit says a-preeeaaach!

I'm gonna preach when the Spirit says a-preeeaaach!"

There is brass and brown sugar in Hibernia's way of delivering this tune. If a Packard could sing, it would sound like this, all shiny and bold and *rolling*.

Everybody is swaying to the beat of this celebration. But the piano lady doesn't look too pleased.

Now comes the third verse, more sassy than the other two.

"I'm gonna shout when the Spirit says a-shooouuut!

I'm gonna shout when the Spirit says a-shooouuut!

I'm gonna shout when the Spirit says a-shooouuut!"

The kids in the choir get to clapping. Hibernia curls her shoulders with a sure rhythm. She presents both her palms, inviting all of us to clap along. Hibernia Lee Tyson owns this song.

Lila's feet are keeping up with the music, and she's singing full out. Lila's nod tells me to join in.

I clap so hard, it hurts. There is a happy, steady stomp dancing its way all over my insides. Everything feels so good from having gladness big in my heart.

Willie's clapping just as much as me. His hands don't even stop him from slipping into the music. The clapping comes so natural. All that puckered skin and his melted-together fingers don't hold Willie back. When I take a good look at Willie's hands, they're freer somehow, ready to rejoice.

Willie says, "Ya girl is fine."

Now Hibernia's voice is ten times higher than cloud nine. She is swinging us to joy's fullest place.

When I look behind me to see who else is taking in our celebration, there is the bleach man, leaning hard in the door to the dayroom. His arms are folded tight. He refuses to clap. But his foot won't obey. It pumps on the floor, following the rhythm of this Easter gift.

After the concert, Willie pulls me over to where Hibernia is standing. He nudges me toward her. "My name's Willie, and *this's* Otis."

I say a soft hello. Then, "I'm glad you sang a solo."

Hibernia plays with the button on her sleeve. "I liked being in the front. I could see you clapping," she says.

My tongue is knotted up tighter than my shoelaces. Hibernia puts her hand to the necklace she's made from her gum-wrapper chain. "This is so pretty," she says.

Willie is quick to say, "Otis made it, and I helped!"

Before I can even say anything, Hibernia is just as quick to speak. "Thank you, Otis. You, too, Willie."

The piano lady comes after Hibernia. I watch her go off with her friends. A brown-skinned girl in a blue dress, her necklace woven from my gum-wrapper chain.

NINE

TEEN DREAMS

May 1937

HiBERNiA

I'M AWAKE AND DRESSED EARLY.

When I get to the parlor, Daddy is holding open the screen door.

"Ready?"

I startle.

"*You're* coming?"

"What rule says I can't?"

Trying to talk Daddy out of anything is impossible. "No rule," I say.

He gives me an up-nod. "Then, come on."

My daddy is a barrel of a man, but that doesn't slow him. His hand swallows mine as he holds on, walking with deliberate steps. Night crawlers can't escape

Daddy's stomp. Neither can the beetles asleep in the grass.

I want to prepare Daddy by telling him I'll be performing Chick Webb's "Harlem Congo" for Joe's Brown Bomber Box Campaign, but he's moving too fast, head forward, with a sure grip on me.

The fairgrounds is a crowded quilt of church hats, suspenders, and babies bundled tight. Morning's sun is just starting its reach. I smell frankfurters. At the central pavilion, where Mr. Haskell usually parks his rations truck, there's a bandstand, with a microphone.

Daddy stops quick, to get his bearings, to figure out where to go.

It's the red-painted sign that shows me the way. "Daddy, over there!"

BROWN BOMBER BOX CAMPAIGN
REGISTRATION

Next to the sign there's a man-size photograph of Joe Louis standing firm, with long, smooth muscles and legs as solid as tree trunks. Joe's dukes are raised to his chin. He's prepared to win.

I like to think that as the reverend's daughter I know most people in Elmira, or at least most people know me. But these are folks from all over, and more kids than I've ever seen in one place.

There's a line to get to the front of the registration table, and bleacher benches for everyone else who's here to watch.

"Go on, register," Daddy says. "I'll be in the stands."

I'm glad to be rid of Daddy. He's messing up my stroll. With him gone, I can weave into the fairgrounds. A long line means nothing to Hibernia Lee. I shoulder-slide through the ribbon of waiting people. Being skinny helps. So does looking at clouds, while you ease your way up. Daydreamers don't get accused of cutting. If anybody notices, I say a simple "Excuse me," mumble an apology for stepping on some toes, and keep sliding.

This morning it works as good as ever. I'm fourth to the front right away, where I see placards for each age category. My eye goes right to "The Twelves." I pick up the registration paper, and scribble my name. As I write, I'm listening and glancing at the other "Twelves" who are warming up. Those kids look like babies, and they *stink* at singing. Even though I'm here to win, I sure don't want to compete with a bunch of off-key whiners.

The next category up is called the "Teen Dreams." It

doesn't take an A-plus student to figure out that the "Teen Dreams" are a whole lot better than "The Twelves."

I fold into the "Teen Dreams" registration line, where I fill out a new paper. I leave the age column blank. Anyone with manners or sense knows it's rude to ask a lady her age, even if she *is* a teen. Or *dreaming* of being a teen. Age is a very private thing. So I am holding on to my privacy, and helping the organizers of the Brown Bomber Box Campaign keep some class in their event.

I'm poker-faced Hibernia when I hand the registration lady my sign-up sheet. She eyes it quickly, studies me, sees that I'm almost as tall as she is, and points me toward the "Teen Dreams."

At the end of the registration table, I pick up my Brown Bomber Box, the cardboard cube that each of us gets for collecting money. My name, like everyone else's, is in big letters on the front. Hibernia is misspelled. The lady has written it from what I scrawled on my registration paper. It says *Nibrenia*. I'm too excited to care. When I do get my name on a real marquee, I'll make sure it's spelled right then.

The contest rules are taped to the box's side. It's simple. We each sing in turn. The audience shows us how much they like our singing by applauding. Then we pass our Brown Bomber Boxes. The true indication of how good we are—and who wins—comes when people put their money in our boxes. Or when they don't. The singer who brings in the most dough for Joe is the winner.

When a kid's Brown Bomber Box goes around and hands stay in pockets, it means the kid's singing is not worth a nickel.

Just like in church. When Daddy gives a good sermon, folks feel inspired, and more coins end up in the collection plate.

This is where I like being the child of a reverend. I understand what it takes to help people part with their cash. Yours Truly is good at *enthusing*.

I find my place among the other "Dreams." As soon as I'm standing next to a girl in a turquoise dress with opals on the collar, and a corsage at her wrist, honey, I know I'm in the right group. *Happy* Hibernia is ready to *enthuse*.

But when I hear this girl warming up, I get something Hibernia Lee Tyson never gets—*nervous!* This "Teen Dream" has some serious lung power. Even when she's just practice singing, I can see by the way she breathes that she's had some kind of formal training.

This girl can *project*. And her hands know how to *express* the notes flying free from her. She's not actually singing; she's *trilling,* and even *that* sounds professional.

"The Twelves" are starting to look better to me, whiny voices and all.

"My name's Carmen," says the girl with the opal collar. "Carmen Bellamy."

I am so busy reconsidering "The Twelves" and picking at my thumbnail that it takes me a moment to see she's trying to shake my hand with her slim fingers.

Carmen. Even her name is high-hat.

"What will you be singing?" she asks. She gestures toward the bandstand microphone.

Only half my attention is working. I'm mostly wishing I had a corsage like hers. I answer by telling her my name. "I'm Hibernia."

The chance to shake Carmen's hand has passed. She's smoothing her hair, fixing her barrette.

"I'm here with my daddy," she says, and points to an eager man down front, a few rows back from the bandstand.

I take this as a chance to look for *my* daddy. Even with so many people, I see him squished between a lady and a little boy in the same row as Carmen's father.

A trumpet blows the start of the contest.

"The Twelves" begin. One by one, they're as pitiful as can be. I watch them pass their Brown Bomber Boxes. Not much coin clinking for any of those whiners. Thank goodness I'm not one of them.

Now it's our turn, the "Teen Dreams."

Carmen goes first. She blows once on her pitch pipe, then collects a rhythm by tap-tapping her foot. This makes me notice her shoes. Real leather, with a heel, and a strap across the ankle. I flinch. Those are *my* shoes from the Sears, Roebuck catalog. Carmen hasn't even started singing, and she's already ahead. Even her toe-rhythm is jazzy.

The beat of her shoe strikes me right away. I *know* that tempo. And here's what else I know. Though I have only heard church folks talk about what a heart attack feels like, I am near to having one.

The sky might as well open up and drop a piano on my head this minute. Carmen is singing "Harlem Congo"! She has stolen my shoes—*and my song!*

She doesn't even need Chick Webb's drum. Her only music is the leather tap of her heel. Her singing rises higher and smoother than an air balloon with a passenger basket.

Carmen's "Congo" is belting off the bandstand, but she's holding down the beat with her foot. The audience is applauding already. Carmen has passed her Brown Bomber Box. Folks are digging for their money.

This is not *happening.*

I am Not-*Happy Hibernia.*

I try to listen politely, but *Not*-Happy Hibernia is getting more *Not*-Happy with each "Congo" beat.

I wish there were another song I could sing. And the truth is, there are lots of them. But I'm not here to sing. I'm here to *siiiing.* "Harlem Congo" is the song to *siiiing.*

I can't take any more of Carmen. If the squeeze on me is any indication, I *will* have a heart attack if I don't *do* something.

My own foot starts a beat of its own, but my poopy, stupid shoes are no match for Carmen's heels.

I look to the photo of Joe Louis and can't believe what I see.

Is there a trick to that picture?

When I fix my eyes on Joe, he *winks at me* from his place on the sign!

I blink to be sure. *I am* not *imagining this.*

Now I know it's time for me to shine.

If this were the ring, Mighty Joe Louis would not stay in his corner. He would go out there and take his prize.

I know every inch of "Harlem Congo." I can feel where it spreads, pumps, syncopates, sizzles.

So I wait. It is so hard to keep still.

I had let my fingernails grow past stubs for this occasion, but hooey to that. I'm chomping as much as I would on an ear of corn.

When Carmen comes to the place where "Harlem Congo" slows its roar, my poopy shoe picks up speed. I double-time with my toe, getting ready to grab the song.

Carmen starts back in, slow to the Congo, then heats up.

I meet her right where she is, at Harlem Congo's hottest place.

I put pepper on that tune.

Carmen glances behind to where I'm standing among the other "Teen Dreams."

Her face has one word written on it: *What?!*

She doesn't stop singing, though. This girl is a pro. Carmen throws down a jam, and takes the Congo up, up, up. She turns the song into locomotion.

I'm at her quick, with slammin' pitch.

The people in the bleachers are calling for my Brown Bomber Box, so I pass it to the front row, and watch lots of pockets turn inside out.

Carmen's ready to put the pulse on this party, and so am I.

She waves me up to where she is on the bandstand. I take my place next to her at the microphone.

Carmen turns her voice into popcorn blips.

I backflip the melody into flatted riffs.

The fairgrounds crowd is on their feet, wanting more.

Daddy's putting two quarters into my Brown Bomber Box and two into Carmen's. When both boxes reach Carmen's daddy, he does the same thing. That's two whole dollars!

Like in church, people are beginning to catch the "giving fever." They are happy to contribute. They're feeling *motivated* to let go of their money, which is not easy in these times.

Carmen and I keeping rolling with the Congo, and soon we're sharing the song.

She bounces me a bop.

I shoot her back a scat.

We are celebrating "Harlem Congo" with ping-pong rhythms.

We are grits with gravy, each bringing out the best in each other.

Happy Hibernia Lee Tyson and Carmen Bellamy are *siiiinging* together.

Our Brown Bomber Boxes are still making their way through the fairgrounds. The contest marshals keep the boxes going and watch so that hobos don't steal the money.

When Carmen and I bring it home with the final Congo groove, the cheers don't stop. I've actually sweat a sheen onto my forehead. I wipe it quick with Thankie Hankie.

For the rest of the morning, kids from "Teen Dreams" sing for Joe. They pass out their Brown Bomber Boxes, but nobody comes close to Carmen and me.

The boxes have all come to the front. The money is being counted.

What happens next is a bigger surprise than a visit from Santa Claus himself. The lady at the registration station comes to the bandstand microphone. "We have a winner," she announces. "And, we have a special guest to broadcast the news live on the radio."

The fairgrounds is as quiet as a library on the day before a spelling test.

I'm back to tapping my poopy shoe, this time from the thing I've been cursed with several times today — rattled nerves.

The registration lady looks to her left at a curtained spot on the bandstand. "Please welcome Skip Gibson from the CBS Radio Network!"

The whole fairgrounds applauds. Some people shout, "Skip! Skip!" Others are truly gasping. I mean, holy cow, it's Skip Gibson, right here in Elmira!

A tall man with creased slacks comes onto the bandstand. The microphone gets louder somehow. "Ladies and gentlemen, I'm Skip Gibson, coming to you live at the Elmira, New York, fairgrounds, one of eight stops on the Mike Jacobs Brown Bomber Box Campaign, where the voices of tomorrow are raising money by singing for Joe Louis."

If it were not rude to interrupt people while they were talking, I would call for Daddy this minute. I would beg Daddy to please take me to a doctor. I know enough now about my heart stopping, and mine has lost its ticker. I am really, really about to have a heart attack.

By this afternoon, Hibernia Lee Tyson will be headline news on the front page of the *Elmira Star-Gazette* as the child who faked being a teen and died of a heart attack at the Elmira fairgrounds.

Skip's delivery is as polished as ever. "The Brown Bomber Box Campaign has raised a lot of cash to keep up Joe's training fees, and to help him get to Comiskey Park next month in Chicago, where he will fight James Braddock for the world heavyweight title."

There are whoops and clapping from all corners of the fairgrounds. Daddy is on his feet, bringing his heavy hands together.

"This was one of the fiercest of all campaign competitions, with two singers leading the pack. The only other times I've seen sparring like today's is in the ring with two fit contenders holding up strong with each other."

More cheers rattle the bleachers.

Skip says, "We saw quite a showing of talent today. Of fortitude, grace, skill, and work."

Carmen and I exchange eager glances.

"There were many boxes stuffed for Joe, and confident voices that sang for Joe's hope. That's what counts most, the solid showing for Joe Louis."

Skip Gibson announces, "*Nibrenia* Lee Tyson, please

come to the microphone." My poopy shoes must be filled with stones. I cannot rise from my chair.

People start to giggle. Skip says, "Carmen Bellamy, will you assist your friend and join her at the front of the bandstand?"

Carmen needs no help. She's got me by the elbow and is propping me next to Skip, who has begun to sing the Joe Louis fight song.

> *"Let's go, mighty Joe.*
> *Battle like the Alamo.*
> *Hey, hey, mighty Joe.*
> *Time to bomb 'em — there you go!*
> *Go, go, mighty Joe!*
> *Get 'em good — there you go."*

The whole fairgrounds joins in, and soon the song becomes a chant:

> *"Go, go, mighty Joe! Get 'em good — there you*
> *go."*

Daddy and Carmen's father are making the most noise.

Carmen and I are bringing it out, too, turning *"Go, go, mighty Joe!"* into harmony.

With everybody cheering for Joe Louis, with Carmen and me leading the way, I start to *siiiing* Joe's name.

I put a spin on the refrain.

> *"Go, go, mighty Joe! Campaign bucks—here you go!"*

The registration lady hands Skip Gibson two Brown Bomber Boxes. Skip holds one up high over his head. The registration lady lifts the other. The box in her hand has Carmen's name on the front. Skip's box says *"Nibrenia* Lee Tyson."

Everyone settles down to hear Skip. "These two singers have brought in the most for Joe. One box is filled with only three dollars more than the other. The two are so close that we've decided to make it even. In the boxing ring we'd call that a draw—a tie."

Carmen hugs me.

"You can sure spark a tune," I say.

"Girl, I need pot holders to handle you."

When Daddy comes to get me at the bandstand, he's brought me a frankfurter.

On the way home, I tell Daddy why I couldn't stand to sing with "The Twelves."

He says, "*Nibrenia,* not even Goliath can stand up to you."

TEN

JOE!

June 22, 1937

WiLLiE

LILA SAY, "DON'T LAG NOW! AND MAKE sure Bird doesn't get away!"

Lila, she's slowing her pace to let us walk ahead. Keeping her eye on us, though. It'll be dark soon.

Otis's got Bird pressed down in the bib of his over-alls. The cat's head is poking up near to Otis's chin. He asking, "Lila, *where* are we going?"

I'm hurrying. Working to keep up.

Otis's got his Philco balanced under one arm. Lila made him bring it. Even though Otis loves his radio, he complaining, saying, "Lila, this isn't fair. My legs can't move so fast. Besides, I need to have my radio turned on at eight o'clock."

We just passed the Mercy gate. Lila, she's stern tonight. "If Mr. Sneed catches us, I will be standing in the unemployment line soon after the sun rises. Hush until we get to Mills Road," she says. "Just walk — don't ask questions."

We follow. Bird's peeking out through the buckle of Otis's overalls.

At the corner of Mills and Sackett, we run into all kinds of folks. They's moving along the street with a purpose. Some's hurrying in little groups. Some's holding pies or cakes. Others is carrying smell-good packages. Fried oxtails, or coleslaw, for sharing with people. Lila's got a jug of lemonade.

All of us along the road wanna be settled before the start-bell rings, especially me.

Otis say, "Lila, do you *know* what tonight is?"

"If we don't get someplace soon, we gonna miss Joe," I say.

"As sure as my name is Lila Weiss, I *know* what this night is. And you can rest assured we will *not* miss the fight between Joe Louis and James Braddock. But what fun is a good fight if you don't share it with friends?"

Otis's whining like a hungry baby wanting milk.

"Lila, we need an outlet for my radio. If we turn back now, we can still tune in on time."

Otis and me, we both slowing down. Lila's moving so fast, we trailing her.

Otis shifts his Philco to under his other arm, then hoists it to his shoulder to get it to balance.

Lila walks backward. She facing us and talking at the same time.

"Boys, you are looking at an old woman with bad joints and a rump that keeps me from moving with any speed. But I am going faster than the two of you put together. And while I suffer from several minor afflictions of the body, I am not senile. I would never ask you to join me as listeners to the biggest prizefight of all time and not think that we just might need a place to plug in your radio. A place that's not near that scab of a man, who, right now, *has* no radio of his own."

I don't talk back. Just pick up my pace to keep up with Lila.

Otis's nodding and smiling. He's hoofing it, too, and looking at Lila with quiet respect.

She say, "So stop moaning, and let's keep hightailing it. Even the cat takes orders better than the two of you."

But Bird's real restless. He's got one paw stretched high out of the overalls bib.

It's getting dark. Nighttime's putting on a cape and sweeping it across the sky. When we pass the fairgrounds and get to Hornby Street, I spot something ahead, flashing. It's mixed with a parade of people, rushing to where they going.

I know that white-white. *Uh-huh,* I know it. That flicker is the fight skirt sash!

"Mama!"

Mama hears me right off. But she's struggling to find me in the jumble of people. "Willie?"

I rush ahead of Lila. I hurry to the voice. I get to where the white-white sash slices at the shadows.

Lila and Otis follow me when they hear me shout again. "Mama! Mama!"

Lila, she back to being ahead of me somehow. She pulling at my wrist. Getting me closer to Mama's calling. *"Willie!"*

But my eye ain't never left looking at the white-white. I been moving in that direction the whole time, till soon I see Mama stopped at a street lamp. She holding a square pan covered with muslin. I push to where Mama waits by a parked car on the corner. She sets the pan down gentle on the car's hood and folds me hard-tight-good into skinny arms that remember how to hug.

Uh-huh! Uh-huh! Uh-huh!

Mama, she don't let go. Same for me. I'm just holding on to Mama. Just holding on.

Here come Lila, and Otis, and Bird to under our street lamp.

I tell Mama, "These's my friends from Mercy."

That's when Mama explains, "I was on my way to Mercy tonight to hear the fight with you, Willie. To come get you, and to bring you home."

I look to Lila. She don't even seem surprised from meeting my mama.

Lila's just smiling and smiling. A knowing kind of smile. A smile when you understand something you already knew, and now it's true 'cause you see it in front of you.

Otis, he the same way. Happy for me. Seeing what he knows already.

I ask Mama, "Where's Sampson?"

"He went to jail for hauling bootleg in the back of his truck."

I let go from hugging Mama. I need to look at her. I need to make sure I'm clear on what she telling me. "Sampson's gone?"

"Locked up tighter than melon rinds in a pickle jar."

Soon as Mama tells me Sampson's locked up, something in me *unlocks*. Something swings open. Same way a door unlatches and lets in light. And right then, my *oh, yeah* is back.

Even with so much happy-for-me, Otis can't help but be eager to keep on.

"The fight'll be starting soon," he say real gentle, careful to not ruin my time with Mama.

Lila invites Mama to come with us.

"I brought some of my corn hash," Mama say. "It's Willie's favorite."

Now we all walk together. The street's getting more quiet. People's mostly settled to where they want to be.

My heart and nerves are a bundle of good-good butterflies, fluttering so free. I carry the pan of hash. I'm smelling its thick sweetness. Feeling Mama in its warmth. I see the True Vine Baptist Church up ahead.

While we walk, Mama say, "You're looking closer to a man than a boy, Willie. Mercy's taken good care of you."

I show Mama my hands. She shakes her head, like she's sad. Kisses what's left of my knuckles.

"I can do good things with these hands," I tell Mama. "I can pull weeds, and even fold gum wrappers to make a chain."

Mama's rubbing on my hands now. I say, "Can hold a fork for eating corn hash with these hands, too." Mama and me, we laugh together, and try to keep up with Lila, who's back to moving fast.

Lila steps to the door and knocks fast. The screen door rattles when her knuckles meet the jamb.

Hibernia answers. I can hear her radio's roar coming from inside. "Lila Weiss, Otis, Willie," Hibernia says, swinging open the door.

I tell Hibernia, "This my mama. She brought her corn hash."

Hibernia's toothy smile say she glad to see us. She don't even bother to ask about Mama. But I notice her taking a fancy to Mama's fight skirt and the white-white sash. Hibernia says, "Get *in* here — quick. The fight's about to start."

Lila say, "We've brought Otis's radio to add to yours. On a night like this, two radios are better than one."

Uh-huh. I got excitement in every bone of my whole body.

Lila lifts the Philco from Otis, plugs it in at an

opposite corner to where Hibernia's radio is set. The whole room fills up with the sound.

Mama and me are holding hands. "Mama," I say, "this is it! Joe's big fight. For the heavyweight championship of the world!"

HiBERNiA

MY FINGERNAILS DON'T STAND A CHANCE.
I've bitten all but one, my left pinkie, down to the skin.
I am saving that final sliver of white for tonight's
fight.

Daddy has moved Speaky from his private room to
our kitchen table. Otis and Willie are here with Lila
Weiss and Daddy and me. They've even brought Willie's mama, a cat, a pan of corn hash, a jug of lemonade,
and a radio of their own.

I remember Daddy telling me about the kids at
Mercy. Some being true orphans. Others living there
because of parents who couldn't take care of them, or
from hard times at home. I don't ask Willie about his

mother. I notice her skirt, though. It's gathered at the waist with a ribbon sash that glints when she moves. I've never seen fabric gleam that way. Up close, it looks like regular cotton. But whenever she turns, even a little, that sash shines like lamé. All of me says, *I want one of those*.

Daddy goes to the larder to get six drinking glasses and some plates, then sets them in front of us on the table. "Sister Weiss," he says, "welcome to you and your friends."

Willie and his mama serve us their corn hash, then slide on the kitchen bench next to me.

Otis gets to the bench from the other side. He says my whole name slowly, like he's enjoying a caramel. *"Hibernia Lee Tyson."*

I like hearing how he says my name. It sounds smooth, like an introduction to a singer at the Savoy.

Quietly I say, "That wrapper chain you made me is sure pretty."

He says, "It looks good on you."

I giggle. "I do look good in jewelry, don't I."

I reach for Lila's lemonade and pour everybody a glass, Otis first. I drink mine down quick.

The cat plunks his paw into my empty glass and licks the lemony drink from his white patch of fur.

"Don't go showing off," says Otis. He sets the cat between me and him on the bench. "Bird," he introduces, "this is Hibernia Lee Tyson."

Otis waves the cat's lemonade paw like it wants to shake my hand. I take the cat's wet mitt in two of my fingers. "Pleased to meet you, cat."

"Bird," Otis corrects me.

Then we hear it—sudden cheering from the spectators at ringside, and Skip Gibson's quicksilver introduction to the fight. I'm so glad to hear Skip's voice. It's a greeting from a friend.

"Ladies and gentlemen, this is Skip Gibson coming to you live from Comiskey Park in Chicago, where I am looking out at forty-five thousand fight fans waiting to see who will be the next heavyweight champion of the world."

All of us scoot toward Speaky. We might as well be a bunch of hairpins, pulled fast by a magnet—the radio. Otis's Philco adds extra boom to the commentary. With so much radio surrounding us, it's as loud as being ringside.

Even Bird's got his ears pricked, and he's up on all fours. I close my eyes to listen. I make what Skip says come into my mind like a moving picture.

"Champion Braddock is wearing the trunks with the white stripes. Joe Louis is wearing the all-dark trunks."

With my eyes shut tight, I say, "All-dark trunks! What kind of star appeal is *that*? Joe, don't you know? A white stripe adds star appeal under bright lights. Braddock is already ahead with the right shorts."

Before I can give Joe any more ideas about his boxing trunks, I am hushed up quick. Daddy and Lila, Otis, Willie, and his mama all pounce on my advice with a firm *"Shhhhh!"*

"But if only Joe just had a little stripe of his own—" I start to defend the importance of trunks with some flash.

Another chorus rings out against me. *"Shhhhhhhhh!"*

I suck my tongue. "You people don't know a thing about show business."

Nobody bothers to hush me again.

Daddy gets up and starts walking the length of our small kitchen. Even with the radio's magnetic power, he can't stay put. His feet make heavy clomps on the floorboards. He lifts the window sash even higher to let in more of the night's breeze.

I start up with my pinkie nail, slowly coaxing it off with tiny little teeth snips.

"Louis looks strong from his corner, eager, like he's ready. Like he's been ready. Braddock, from his corner, is quietly confident. They enter the ring."

Lila pours her second glass of lemonade.

Willie's got Bird now and is hugging him close. The cat fights Willie's hold. He wants to nose the radio. Otis knuckles Bird's head softly. "Easy now," he says.

Daddy fiddles with the radio's tuning knob. He turns up the volume almost to its fullest.

I bite down hard on my nail. I start to tear it away from the skin. Otis gently draws my pinkie from my clamped teeth. I'm grateful for the favor. Anything to save my nails.

Out from the radio the start bell rings.

Something in me is ringing, too. It's not a bell, though. The *ding, ding, ding* comes from a single place inside my chest.

It's a signal that tells me I'm at a beginning.

WiLLiE

"BRADDOCK COMES OUT PUNCHING! HE'S trying to take Louis by surprise. He's looking to land right-hand punches. Louis jabs and moves back. We're only minutes into round one and Louis is showing signs of retreating. This isn't like the Brown Bomber."

We all eating Mama's corn hash and, oh, is it ever good. Every part of me is tight. Fixed hard as the lid on a jar filled with firecrackers. I'm holding in so much. Ready to bust. My Saint Christopher medal is hot from me pressing on it. From aching for Joe to win. *Saint Christopher, protect me from myself. Drive away the hurt I feel, just from* thinking *Joe could lose.*

Call me a sissy. Say I'm a milksop. I'm wearing Saint Christopher like a necklace worth a fortune.

"Louis lands a right to the side of Braddock's head. But the champ is back fast with a short uppercut to Joe's jaw. Louis's legs give way! He lands on the canvas! He's down!"

"Joe, get up! Get up, Joe!" I holler at the radio. I press Saint Christopher to me. Maybe it can keep my stuttering heart from jumping to the floor.

Bird pounces at the radio. Otis scoops him back from the speaker holes. Otis, he's hollering, loud as me. *"Joe!"*

"Louis recovers quickly. He's back on his feet! But Braddock is at him, throwing right-handed haymakers! Louis lands a left hook and a right cross. Braddock looks hurt. And there's the bell—the end of round one!"

My breath comes short and shaky. It's a wonder I can breathe at all. I'm blowing through puffed cheeks.

Between rounds there's an advertisement for Ivory Soap. I eat more corn hash and wash it back with some of the lemonade while we waiting for round two. "Careful," Mama say. "If you eat too fast, you'll get a stomachache." I slow down, glad I got a ma here to badger me.

The start bell clangs.

"Braddock comes out of his corner hepped for action. He throws right hand after right hand. Braddock is a wild animal tonight. He won't let up. And the Brown Bomber is not fighting at his best."

My head's in both my hands. I can't even *look* at the radio. *Uh-uh,* can't even watch what I'm hearing. My heart's a brick. *Uh-huh,* I'm as sissy as they come. I bite the walls of my mouth to keep from being a crybaby.

Saint Christopher, help me. Help Joe.

None of us says nothing.

Lila's hands is wrung together.

Hibernia grabs on to her daddy.

I ain't letting go of Mama.

Me and Otis share a sad sideways glance.

Otis gives Bird to me. Me and Mama hold him close. My cat's trembling.

I shut my eyes and think heavy on something Mama once told me. Mama, she must be some kind of mind reader. She says what I'm thinking. She calls it out to the radio: "Joe, don't give up five minutes before a miracle happens."

I set Bird in my lap, so's I can go back to my medal. But I'm more than rubbing on Saint Christopher now. I squeeze that tinny charm so hard, I'm near to crushing it. And *uh-huh,* I'm a crybaby milksop, 'cause all I can say to Saint Christopher is *"Please!"*

I can't stay in my chair. Mama's the first to notice me rocking. She takes Bird, and I'm up.

I claw-punch in front of me. Dancing back on my feet to the corner where Otis's radio is parked. I *hook, cross.* Go strong for a jaw.

Jab. Cut. Duck. Call, "Joe! Joe! Joe!"

And five minutes pass. And here comes a miracle!

Round three: *"Louis catches Braddock with a left that tears open the champ's lip!"*

Round four: *"Braddock is bleeding bad!"*

Round five: *"A solid left by Joe Louis rips open another cut, this time on the left side of his rival's forehead! The champ is slowing down. But the Brown Bomber is on the up-and-up!"*

It's as if a mighty hand is yanking the room to its feet. Everybody else jumps to stand.

"Yes!" shouts the reverend. But he's fast to hush so's we can hear the rest.

By round six, faith is here like a long-gone friend. It's getting easier to pull breath. I'm still pushing air through rounded cheeks. But it's from relief, not upset.

"Joe comes on strong against his foe. Braddock tries to keep the battle going, but he's struggling."

The reverend turns up the radio. Skip Gibson, he sounding like he trusts in Mama's belief about miracles coming soon.

"As we wind down the seventh round, Joe's rights don't let up, and Jimmy Braddock starts to retreat. Louis powers a left hook. Braddock staggers! There's the bell. Braddock is saved for the moment."

We back to sitting. Otis say, "It's not over till it's over."

That's the hard truth of prizefighting. Nobody's a winner till somebody's a winner. At round eight, all of us got our ears pinned to the radio.

"There's the bell. Braddock tries a right hand, but Louis is faster, stronger. He hits Braddock with his right hand. Now Louis has got his left at work. He pops Braddock with a left to the jaw, then hooks his left to Jimmy's head. There's another bruise now over the champ's left eye! Braddock is reaching for anything he can to keep from falling. He throws a sloppy right! He misses! A dynamite right from Joe — a hard blow to Braddock's chin — brings Braddock tumbling to the canvas! The champ falls forward on his face!"

Otis and me let out noises that are hoots and roars, all rolled into one.

The girls got their own ways of shouting good news. "Hot-doo!" Lila hollers.

"*Double*-hot-doo!" Hibernia yells.

"Hash-hot!" shouts Mama.

Skip Gibson tells America, *"Joe Louis goes to a neutral corner. Referee Tommy Thomas is over Braddock. He starts to count. One . . . two . . . three . . ."*

Mama and me count with Tommy Thomas. Otis and Hibernia count with Tommy and Mama and me. Lila and Hibernia's daddy both got their heads down. They's saying the numbers silently.

The world's counting *". . . four . . . five . . ."*

Nobody's a winner till somebody's a winner.

"Braddock is stunned," says Skip. *"He struggles to a sitting position. He's trying to get up. . . ."*

Otis

"SIX...SEVEN...EIGHT...BRADDOCK CAN'T rouse *himself. He's out cold from the Brown Bomber's thunderous right punch!*"

I'm wishing on Joe, talking to Daddy and Ma quietly in my mind.

Shake on a promise.

All of me is more jittery than a croaker from a pond springing to the finish line in a frog-jumping contest.

Before the count even gets to ten, I take Hibernia by both her hands, and we're off that kitchen bench fast as jackrabbits. She's doing a jig step, showing me how to be her partner.

"Joe Louis has scored a devastating knockout over Jimmy Braddock to win the heavyweight championship of the world!"

Hibernia's daddy stomps his iron foot. "Hoooeeee!"

Outside, hollers fill up the night with folks in the street and on the rooftops calling, "Joe! Joe! Joe!"

Pots and pans rattle and clank, playing the music of victory.

Willie makes the chant his own. *"My Joe! My Joe!"* His fists punch at the place above his head.

We are all hugging and laughing and doing a ring-around-the-rosy dance. Bird is frisking at the center of our circle. And I swear that cat's tiny lips are pressed into a kitty grin.

I look to see if I'm still stepping on the floor. Or are my feet riding on some kind of joy-wind?

I wrap my hand over Hibernia's. "Let me hold that for you," I say. Hibernia presses her hand in mine, gentle and firm at the same time.

I wish Daddy and Ma were here to dance and ride with me. I try to swallow back the hard spot at the base of my throat, but it's stronger than I am.

Lila's eyes are wet. So are Willie's and his ma's, and Hibernia's, too. And the reverend, he's wiping at *his* eyes with the back of his big hand.

Everything's mixed up and blurry from happy crying that won't quit. But I am clear on knowing one thing. There's no more yesterday. There isn't even tomorrow. All I have is now. Here. With Lila, Willie and his ma, Bird, Hibernia Lee Tyson, her daddy, and *two* radios.

And Joe Louis. The Brown Bomber. Giving us brightness and hope.

We settle at the table.

Hibernia pours the last of the lemonade.

Willie serves more of his ma's hash.

I say a riddle.

"What makes you feel strong and weak at the same time?"

Lila says, "Love."

AUTHOR'S NOTE

Joseph Louis Barrow (May 13, 1914–April 12, 1981) was a strong and beautiful symbol of hope. He was born the seventh of eight children to Alabama sharecroppers and grew up to become one of the most noted athletes of his day, the world heavyweight boxing champion from 1937 to 1949.

Hailed for his pounding punches and focused fighting, Louis was called the "Brown Bomber" for his smooth, dark complexion and his crushing right-and-left-hand combination blows. When Joe Louis defeated James J. Braddock on June 22, 1937, to become the heavyweight champion of the world, the event instilled overwhelming pride in the hearts of African Americans and served as an important moment in boxing history. On the night of this fight against Braddock, African Americans were so filled with excitement that many celebrated until dawn the next day.

In his autobiography entitled *I Wonder as I Wander,* Langston Hughes, the noted Harlem Renaissance poet and writer, describes Louis's victory this way:

> *Each time Joe Louis won a fight in those depression*
> *years, even before he became champion, thousands*
> *of colored Americans on relief or W.P.A., and poor,*
> *would throng out into the streets all across the land*
> *to march and cheer and yell and cry because of Joe's*
> *one-man triumphs. No one else in the United States*
> *has ever had such an effect on Negro emotions — or*
> *on mine. I marched and cheered and yelled and*
> *cried, too.*

On June 22, 1938, the Brown Bomber returned to the ring with German fighter Max Schmeling to avenge his 1936 loss to him. The highly publicized fight represented so much more than a boxing match. As Adolf Hitler's Nazi Germany carried out a campaign to create a master white Aryan race that excluded Jews, Gypsies, people with disabilities, and anyone else it did not like, Joe served as an example of America's powerful democracy. (During a visit by Louis to the White House just before the Schmeling fight, President Franklin D. Roosevelt squeezed Joe's arm and said, "We're depending on those muscles for America.")

In his second fight with Max Schmeling, Joe Louis knocked out Schmeling in the first round, further establishing himself as an American hero.

Joe Louis retired as heavyweight boxing champion in March 1949. He came out of retirement to defend his title against Ezzard Charles in New York City in September 1950 but lost the match.

The radio commentary throughout this novel is taken from recordings of actual broadcasts of Joe Louis fights. Skip Gibson and Rusty Donovan are fictional characters drawn from several boxing commentators of the time. The facts about Joe Louis and the fight details are true. They really happened as described by the radio commentary in this book. Additional factual information was obtained through extensive research of boxing and sports history and the use of primary source materials, including interviews with newspaper writers, boxing memorabilia, and historical research about the radio medium during the Great Depression.

The song "Let's Go, Mighty Joe" is derived from an actual Joe Louis campaign jingle, played on the radio to promote Joe Louis fights.

While this novel is based on facts, *Bird in a Box* is a work of fiction. This book started with a story told to me by my late maternal grandmother, Marjorie Frances Williams. "Gam," as we called her, loved to talk about her father, George "Cyclone" Williams, a local amateur prizefighter who, as a teenager, boxed in Elmira, New York, and other small towns in the Chemung County region of New York State. Cyclone, my great-grandfather, was known by the local press as "Elmira's Sensational Battler." A devoted Joe Louis fan, he became my character Willie Martel.

When I was the age Hibernia is in this story, my mother—who spent part of her childhood in a Depression-era orphanage—told me how important Joe Louis's victories had been for African Americans. As a young girl, I enjoyed family gatherings, listening to adults recalling the night Joe Louis nabbed the world heavyweight championship title. My mother described how she felt as a girl herself, seeing grown men and women crying tears of joy at the stunning achievement of a black mother's son.

This novel's remaining characters—Otis, Hibernia, Lila, and the reverend—are derived from other family members and their shared experiences.

The Mercy Home for Negro Orphans is a fictional place based on the orphanage where my mother stayed for a time. The True Vine Baptist Church is a fictional depiction of the church my mother attended as a child living in Elmira.

My father also grew up in Elmira, in a family with limited means. His father left the family to find work in cities outside Elmira. My grandfather worked away from his loved ones, like Otis's daddy.

The Claremont Hotel was not in Philadelphia, though it is a common hotel name.

The Brown Bomber Box Campaign is also fiction, informed by the marketing and promotion smarts of boxing manager Mike Jacobs, who often found unconventional and inventive ways to raise Joe Louis's profile with the public.

Inspired by this and other true events, *Bird in a Box* is mostly a book about the power of the human spirit, and how one man's triumph brought glory to so many people.

—Andrea Davis Pinkney

REAL PEOPLE AND PLACES IN *BIRD IN A BOX*

The Apollo Theater. Constructed in 1914 on Harlem's 125th Street, the Apollo Theater featured live stage shows, often introducing new singers who later would go on to become famous. The theater quickly became known as the place "where stars are born and legends are made." Ella Fitzgerald got her start at the Apollo as one of the first winners of the popular Amateur Nite at the Apollo talent contests. The Apollo still features up-and-coming singers and is one of Harlem's noted historic landmarks.

Max Baer (1909–1959). Known as "Madcap Maxie," Baer was one of the most charismatic boxers of his time. Folks admired Baer for his movie-star good looks and his showmanship in the ring. He was hailed as having one of the hardest punches in heavyweight history. After retiring from boxing, Baer became a screen, radio, and vaudeville actor. Baer was the father of Max Baer Jr., also an actor, known for his role as Jethro on the popular sixties television series *The Beverly Hillbillies.*

Jack Benny (1894–1974). Jack Benny was a vaudeville stage performer who later became a national radio personality with *The Jack Benny Program,* a weekly radio show that ran from 1932 to 1948 on NBC and from 1949 to 1955 on CBS. Benny was popular for his comedy routines that often took everyday situations and made them funny. After his radio show, he hosted a popular television program.

James Braddock (1905–1974). James Walter Braddock was known for his powerful right-handed punch, though his boxing career went through several ups and downs. Like many during the Great Depression, Braddock struggled to support his family, and his responsibilities often took him away from boxing. He suffered from injuries to his hands, which also affected his ability to fight consistently. Because of his skill in winning fights in which he was the underdog, Braddock gained the nickname "Cinderella Man."

Duke Ellington (1899–1974). Edward Kennedy Ellington, called the "King of the Keys" by his fans, was a world-renowned jazz pianist. In 1927 Duke Ellington and His Orchestra began a highly successful run at Harlem's Cotton Club. He also played at the Savoy Ballroom. Ellington was a leader in swing jazz, and through a career that spanned fifty years, he wrote, produced, and performed thousands of compositions, many of which became hits that remain popular today. These include "Caravan," "Sophisticated Lady," and "It Don't Mean a Thing (If It Ain't Got That Swing)."

Ella Fitzgerald (1917–1996). Ella Jane Fitzgerald never knew her father and suffered the death of her mother when she was a teenager. Soon afterward, Ella joined the Chick Webb Orchestra. Under Chick's care, Ella's career soared. She became a vocal virtuosa, best known for her scat singing. She went on to become one of the leading ladies of jazz, winning more than a dozen Grammy Awards, and in 1979 was named by President Jimmy Carter as one of the most talented American performers who ever lived.

Mike Jacobs (1880–1953). Boxing promoter Michael Strauss Jacobs is said to have been the most powerful promoter in the sport from the mid-1930s until he retired in 1946. Though he was well known in boxing circles, Jacobs' career took a dramatic turn in 1935 when he met with the managers of Joe Louis, who was an up-and-coming heavyweight contender at that time. Louis had been managed by a group of men from his hometown of Detroit, Michigan, but chose to work with Jacobs as his boxing career gained momentum. The hiring of a private railroad car to take Joe on a tour of exhibition matches really happened. "The Brown Bomber Box Campaign" is a fictional creation, though Jacobs advanced Joe's profile and fame in many creative ways. It was Mike Jacobs who promised a heavyweight champion title shot to Louis at a time when racial barriers kept black boxers from obtaining a world championship. In 1982 Jacobs was posthumously elected to the World Boxing Hall of Fame, and the International Boxing Hall of Fame in 1990.

Bob Pastor (1914–1996). Born in New York City, Pastor was a boxer who became famous for entering the ring twice against heavyweight champion Joe Louis. Pastor was enrolled in New York University, but he gave up college to pursue his career as a fighter. In sixty-five bouts from 1935 to 1942, he had a record of 53–7–5, with seventeen knockouts. Pastor had one fight for the heavyweight title, when he went up against Joe Louis in Detroit on September 20, 1939. After retiring from boxing, Pastor joined the Army, where he trained ski troops.

Charlie Retzlaff (1904–1970). Known by his fans as "The Duluth Dynamiter," Retzlaff was a heavyweight professional boxer from Duluth, Minnesota, who remained undefeated through his first twenty-one fights.

The Savoy Ballroom. Located in Harlem on Lenox Avenue between 140th and 141st Streets, the Savoy was a popular nightclub and dance spot from 1926 to 1958. Known as "The Home of Happy Feet" by those who frequented the dance floor, the Savoy also featured live jazz orchestra performances and vocal selections that were broadcast live for radio audiences. *Swing Time at the Savoy* is a fictional radio show name, though each week radio listeners could tune in to enjoy an array of selections coming from the ballroom.

Max Schmeling (1905–2005). German boxer Maximillian Adolph Otto Siegfried Schmeling fought Joe Louis on two occasions. Both fights brought boxing to international attention, because of their social and political significance when the Nazi regime in Germany was at its height. Schmeling was never a supporter of the Nazi party, but he cooperated with the government's efforts to soften negative views of the Nazis. However, it later became known that Schmeling risked his life to save the lives of two Jewish children in 1938. Schmeling was heavyweight boxing champion of the world between 1930 and 1932.

Jack Sharkey (1902–1994). Born Joseph Paul Zukauskas in Binghamton, New York, Jack Sharkey had solid success in the ring. In an effort to gain more publicity, Zukauskas came up with the stage name Jack Sharkey by combining the names of two of his idols, heavyweight boxing icons Jack Dempsey and Tom Sharkey. Sharkey was a daring fighter who often took on opponents who had more experience than he did. He was the only man with few boxing credentials who was brave enough to face two reputable opponents—prizefighters Jack Dempsey and Joe Louis.

Madam C. J. Walker (1867–1919). Born Sarah Breedlove, Madam C. J. Walker was an entrepreneur who became the first black female millionaire. Walker built an empire by developing and marketing a line of hair-care products for African American women. Walker was also known for her civil rights activism and her philanthropy, leaving two-thirds of her estate to educational institutions and charities, including the NAACP, the Tuskegee Institute, and Bethune-Cookman College.

Fats Waller (1904–1943). Thomas "Fats" Waller was a pianist, bandleader, and jazz musician known for playing stride piano (a jazz piano style) and organ music. He was the son of the pastor of Harlem's well-attended Abyssinian Baptist Church, where he learned to play the organ. Waller is best known for his recordings of the jazz hits "Honey-suckle Rose" and "Ain't Misbehavin'."

Chick Webb (birth year disputed–1939). William Henry "Chick" Webb was a leader in swing jazz. He was born somewhere between 1902 and 1909. As a child, Chick contracted spinal tuberculosis, which stunted his growth and left him with little use of his legs. He was less than five feet tall, but he took the music world by storm with his drumming. In 1927, at the suggestion of Duke Ellington, Webb formed a quintet called the Harlem Stompers. He started playing at the Savoy Ballroom, where crowds came to hear his flamboyant drum rhythms. In 1931, he formed the Chick Webb Orchestra. The band became the house band for the Savoy, with such songs as "Stompin' at the Savoy," "If Dreams Come True," and "Blue Lou." The song "Harlem Congo" was arranged by guitarist Charlie Dixon. It was recorded in November 1937 after it had gained popularity from being performed by Ella Fitzgerald in front of live audiences and played on the radio several months before.

RESOURCES

For further enjoyment:

Adler, David A.
Joe Louis: America's Fighter.
New York: Harcourt, 2005.

Bak, Richard.
Joe Louis: The Great Black Hope.
Boulder, CO: Taylor Trade Publishing, 1995.

Hughes, Langston.
I Wonder as I Wander - An Autobiographical Journey.
New York: Hill and Wang, 1993.

Libby, Bill.
Joe Louis, The Brown Bomber.
New York: Lothrop, Lee & Shepard Books, 1980.

Lipsyte, Robert.
Joe Louis, A Champ for All America.
New York: HarperCollins Publishers, 1994.

Margolick, David.
*Beyond Glory: Joe Louis vs. Max Schmeling,
and a World on the Brink.*
New York: Knopf, 2005.

Mead, Chris.
Champion — Joe Louis, Black Hero in White America.
New York: Scribner, 1985.

Myler, Patrick.
Ring of Hate: Joe Louis vs. Max Schmeling:
The Fight of the Century.
New York: Arcade Publishing, 2006.

Video:
HBO Sports Presents: Boxing's Best.

Video:
The Great Depression & The New Deal.
Schlessinger Media,
United States History Video Collection, 2003.

Video:
The Joe Louis Story.
Xenon Entertainment Group, 1992.

DISCUSSION GUIDE

1. List what you've learned about Hibernia Lee Tyson. Circle the top three things about her that you believe are the most important to the story.

2. Decide what are the three most important facts about Willie's life. Discuss your choices.

3. What are some things that make Otis feel better? What do you do to feel better? Who takes care of you when you feel bad?

4. Describe Hibernia's relationship with her father. Does he seem strict to you or not? What, if anything, do they have in common?

5. Why does Otis's dad move to Philadelphia without his family? What does he ask Otis to do for him?

6. Why does Willie let Ricky Tate knock him out with one punch even though he loves to box?

7. What happens when Otis's dad comes home from Philadelphia to visit the family?

8. Describe the incident that forces Willie to leave his home and arrive at Mercy. Why does his mother stay? What are the long-term effects of this incident on Willie?

9. True Vine Baptist Church is like a second home to Hibernia. What does Hibernia like most about church? Who joins the congregation, and what does she ask of the pastor?

10. Describe Mr. Sneed and Mrs. Weiss's argument as Otis overhears it. Whose philosophy do you agree with more? Which one do most of your teachers subscribe to?

11. How does the radio become a connection between Otis and Willie? What does it offer to each boy? Is there anything in your life that is as important as the radio?

12. What does Hibernia discover in her father's Bible? How does it make her feel? What do you think she should do?

13. Lila shares the three S's for gift giving—sincere, soon, and sweet. Do you agree with her? How does Otis's attempt to use it on Hibernia work out?

14. What does Willie find on Christmas Eve? In what ways would you compare him to what he found?

15. Over time, Willie learns to expand the use of his hands. What two things does he learn that help him?

16. Why does Mr. Sneed snatch the Philco from Otis and Willie? How is he repaid for his cruelty? How is it eventually recovered?

17. Describe what happens at the Brown Bomber's Box Campaign. Does this event change Hibernia's relationship with her father? What does she learn?

18. Why is the career of Joe Louis so important to the African American community? Is boxing more than just a sporting event or not? Why? How does it bring all the characters in the novel together?

19. In the end, what happens to each of our characters? Predict where each of them will be in five years. What about in ten? What evidence from the novel makes you think this?

ACKNOWLEDGMENTS

Writing a novel is like calling folks to a sewing circle and asking each of them to stitch their own unique patches into the quilt you envision. I was blessed with the guidance and advice of many wonderful people who helped me bring *Bird in a Box* to fruition by lending their time and expertise, and by each providing an important stitch to this book's tapestry.

I wish to thank Richard Holbrook and Richard Weigle, librarians at New York City's Paley Center for Media (formerly the Museum of Television and Radio), for allowing me to spend countless hours in the center's media library archive listening to commentary of Joe Louis fights and for directing me to the proper chronology of boxing matches and those that were the most pivotal in Joe Louis's career. Thank you, Rachel Dworkin, archivist at the Booth Library, Chemung County Historical Society, for helping me to reconnect with Cyclone Williams through his photographs and letters. Thank you, Joe Mink, sports reporter from the *Elmira Star-Gazette,* whose writings offered valuable source material on the boxing history of Elmira, New York. True appreciation goes to Craig Hamilton of Jo Sports, Inc., an expert in the field of boxing memorabilia, for finding me a pair of authentic boxing gloves from the late 1930s that I now own and cherish, and for showing me a pair of the actual boxing gloves worn by Joe Louis.

Thank you to the late John Keats, from Syracuse University's Newhouse School of Public Communications, for reading so many drafts of my works and for offering me one-on-one editing tutorials and advice on the crafting of a novel. Thank you, Keats, for always having an open door.

Rebecca Sherman of Writers House, you are a beacon of good sense, keen editorial insight, and grace. I extend heartfelt thanks to Megan Tingley and everyone at Little, Brown Books for Young Readers, especially to my tremendous editor, Alvina Ling, and also Connie Hsu, for reading countless drafts and revisions, for always coming to me with brilliant ideas for making *Bird in a Box* better each time, and for encouraging me to dig a little deeper into the novel's essence and characters. I am appreciative of the fact-checking research assistance of Elizabeth Segal and of the copyediting talents of Pamela Marshall and Marie Salter, who each brought clarity and correctness to the facts and word usage throughout the book.

Thanks to Saho Fujii, for conceiving and designing a gorgeous book jacket. And thank you to Sean Qualls, for bringing my characters to visual life with your evocative illustrations.

The fellowship of writers is an essential tool for an author. Thank you, Marilyn Nelson, and everyone at the Soul Mountain writers' retreat in East Haddam, Connecticut, for allowing me to inhabit your sacred walls so that I could escape my city life to find the quiet needed for writing and editing.

As an author of historical fiction, I spend countless hours at the library, reading, researching, refining, discovering. I wish to thank those librarians who, through the years, have been "book angels," providing me with spot-on information and going to the ends of the earth to help me nail the research materials I need. Thank you to my late friend, historian Susan Snedeker, for reading each and every word of my books and for always knowing exactly where to find the correct historical reference information to flesh out my stories.

When writing historical fiction based on one's family, relatives are invaluable. Thank you to my aunt Rosa and uncle Darryl Clark, for first introducing me to the photograph of boxer Cyclone Williams and for igniting my interest in his story. Thanks to my cousin, historian and newspaper reporter, Larry Ransey, for sleuthing out facts about Elmira's boxing history and the history of African

American boxers in the upstate and central New York regions. Deep gratitude to my late grandmother, Marjorie Frances Williams, for rounding out the story of Cyclone's life and aspirations. To my mother, Gwendolyn Davis, and to my late father, Philip J. Davis, thank you for sharing so many stories from our family tree, for providing colorful details of your lives during the Great Depression, and for always encouraging me to share stories with others.

To my children, Chloe and Dobbin, thank you for your continued patience and understanding as Mom spends so many hours glued to her writing desk. And to both of you, for being such astute readers and for offering me your opinions on what works and what doesn't.

To my incredible husband and soul mate, Brian Pinkney, thank you, my darling, for granting me the time and space to create. Thank you for keeping our kids fed, entertained, happy, and busy on Sundays and late nights when I desperately needed to write, and for allowing me to swim to my heart's content so that I could enter "the zone" required for crafting a book of this length. Without you, no quilt is worth stitching.

Christine Simmons

ANDREA DAViS PiNKNEY

is the *New York Times* bestselling author of more than twenty books for children, including *Sit-In*, one of many collaborations with her husband, illustrator Brian Pinkney. They live in Brooklyn, New York, with their two children.